Christmas Under the Yellow Pine

A Christmas Compendium

Michael Kinnett

SR Staley

Saundra G. Kelley

Diane Sawyer

Published by:
Southern Yellow Pine (SYP) Publishing
4351 Natural Bridge Rd.
Tallahassee, FL 32305

www.syppublishing.com

This is a work of fiction. Names, characters, places, and events that occur either are the products of the author's imagination or are used fictitiously. Any resemblance to actual persons, places, or events is purely coincidental.

The contents and opinions expressed in this book do not necessarily reflect the views and opinions of Southern Yellow Pine Publishing, nor does the mention of brands or trade names constitute endorsement.

ISBN-13: 978-1-59616-116-0
ISBN-13: ePub 978-1-59616-117-7

Printed in the United States of America
First Edition
November 2020

Table of Contents

The Gift of Charity

Michael Kinnett

The stories I've told up till now were from the journals of the Kohler and Agnusdei families. The journal of Michael Brandon Kohler I presented under the title, *Apalachicola Pearl*. The second journal, the writings of LaRaela Retsyo Agnusdei, known as Pearl, I presented under the title, *Apalachicola Gold*, and *Apalachicola Mother of Pearl* were the writings of Olivia Agnusdei Harris, the daughter of Pearl. In his journal, Michael Brandon Kohler compared history to the Apalachicola River, "for just as the water of our river is connected to all the waters of the world, so does all of history share a connection. To find these histories, one must look beyond the family Bible to places where our pasts collided and touched the lives of others. It is in the writing of others that we gain true insight into our legacies."

Three volumes and I have only scratched the surface. A person's life consists of many stories, all happening at the same time. Some of the stories in the journals didn't support the original storyline and I chose to omit them. These omissions should not be misconstrued in any way that might diminish their importance. Today I'd like to share one of these stories. Recorded in the journals, and taking place during the same time period, this story is also of a great treasure. Taken in part, from the writing of the Vicar, Horace Rutledge. I hope you enjoy, *"The Gift of Charity,"* a story of riches not made of gold.

******

By no fault of her own, Charity was cursed with beauty, sentencing her to a life of misuse and abuse. She was not sent to the fields; chosen instead to labor in a great house of the south where she drew the unwanted attentions of her Master. Although looking back, she felt fortunate when at thirteen she found true love, if even for a short time. She'd allowed this love into her life, knowing all too well they'd soon be parted, but that was a long time ago.

Charity, purchased at the age of fourteen, was one of thirty-five slaves belonging to Mr. Thomas Orman. She lived in a slave shack behind the Orman's house in the delta town of Apalachicola, Florida. She had borne four children—her master Mr. Thomas believed they were all his children, but unknown to Orman, she was with child, showing no signs when she was purchased. He had assumed the boy was his, and she saw no benefit in his knowing any different.

In later years, Orman was surprised when Charity produced enough money to buy her son's freedom. That son, Matthew, became a free black minister tending to the spiritual needs of plantation slaves. It was through Charity that Matthew's father passed the money need to purchase his son's freedom. The father, hiding in plain sight, waited, praying for change, in the hope of someday embracing his family. Her second boy, Mark, died of the fever at the age of two. Her third son, Luke, was sold at the age of six, creating a great sadness in her life. She'd had no word of him since that terrible day. Her baby boy, John Milton Orman, known to most as Milton, traveled with Thomas Orman's white son, William Thomas Orman, attending to his needs during The Terrible War.

Thomas only had one son by his wife. Although Mrs. Sarah Orman knew his attentions to Charity were forced, Charity felt

4

it was natural for Mrs. Orman to feel some resentment toward her and her children, but for the most part, their relationship remained amicable. This practice was common on plantations and the wives were expected to overlook their husband's indiscretions if they wanted to maintain their status. Orman's granddaughter, Sarah Genevieve, known to most as Miss Sadie, was well educated and accepting of a change in regards to slavery. She felt great affection toward Miss Charity who had raised her and her father, William, as well. It was behind closed doors that she and her father displayed affection for their black family. It was Miss Charity's good fortune that through time and labor, her beauty faded, no longer attracting the Master's eye.

Faithful and loyal Charity's spirit transcended the horrors of slavery as she sought a modicum of happiness in a life of hard labor. She was comforted by an unwavering faith in her God, knowing at the end of her labors Heaven eternal waited, and she'd walk in glory with her Christ.

Recently, the Vicar asked her for help with a little girl in need, and Charity's heart went out to this little girl. Generous to a fault, Charity was always there for those in need. She was locally known for her treatment of those cancers that afflicted the shut-ins and was often rented out by Orman to care for those in need. Amused, the Vicar described his first meeting with Pearl to Miss Charity, but because Pearl's recollection of events made me smile, I chose instead to quote Pearl's account.

******

"I remember the first time I stood with my mouth gaping open, looking up at the pillars of the Trinity Episcopal Church. I was drawn by unknown forces to enter the sanctuary. With eyes as big as saucers, I tried to comprehend the majesty of this

5

palace. I fully expected God himself to enter from the back and ask me what I was doing there.

Trinity Episcopal Church, Apalachicola, Florida

Suddenly, there was a sound so loud and so deep my teeth vibrated in my head. My eyes shifted to colossal pipes running clear to the top of the great hall. That was when I noticed an old man smiling and peeking around a large wooden box. I just knew it had to be him—God.

My voice was silenced, and my bare feet held fast to the floor as God stood and approached down the center aisle. Overwrought, I stood in the presence of God and fainted.

When my eyes once again opened, I just knew I had been transported to heaven. I lay on a bench with my head resting on God's lap, looking up through the branches of a live oak tree. God had one hand on the back of the bench and in the other was holding and reading from a copy of the book he had written called, "The Bible." God looked down on me kindly. "Are you alright child?" he asked.

"Yes, God," I responded.

Noticeably amused, he smiled. "I'm not God, child, but I do work for him. You can call me Vicar."

Sitting up, I asked, "Is Vicar your whole name?"

"Well not really; my given name is Horace Rutledge, but people just call me Vicar because that's who I am when I work for God," said the Vicar.

"Pleased to meet you, Vicar." I boldly extended my hand to shake. Once again, the Vicar was noticeably amused. I told him, "I understand about your name; you and I have the same kinda' problem. My real name is LaRaela Retsyo Agnusdei, but everybody calls me Pearl…, but I don't work for God."

I didn't understand why, but the Vicar began laughing out loud, and his eyes started watering as though he was crying. Eventually, he calmed himself, and the first thing he did was give me a big hug and thank me for nothing.

This would be the first of many visits to my new friend the Vicar. He was a good man who helped me with my reading and writing, and he was always full of good advice.

During our visits, I tried to explain to the Vicar Rutledge that hunger is a good teacher when it comes to rolling drunks and picking pockets. I told him the pain of hunger was stronger than the inner voice of the conscience he kept talking about. He spent the afternoon trying to convince me otherwise. I eventually relented just to let him off the hook.

******

Charity had seen this little slip of girl sneaking into town down the path behind her shack and had wondered where she came from, and how she even survived back in the wetland. The path itself ended in little more than a swamp and was a haven for all kinds of venomous creatures not to mention the many large gators that called it home. Not meaning to be deceitful, she devised a plan to meet this waif on her terms. If the Vicar's feelings were right about this child, and they usually were, if she truly possessed a good heart, she would soon find a valued friend in Miss Charity.

The girl was small for her age and wise beyond her years according to the Vicar. One day after Charity saw her pass by, she wandered down through the wetlands and was surprised to find a small dingy tied up in the tall grass. To judge her by her size, she should still have been cared for and playing with dolls, but instead, she was rowing in, from God only knows where, and spending her days in town.

Even before the Vicar asked for help, she had worried over this child, having seen her pass behind her shack to wander the streets in town. But it was not wise for a slave to engage in conversation with any white, let alone a white child. It had been a few months since Pearl's arrival, and in that short time, she had become a fixture in Apalachicola, appearing in different places and engaging anyone who walked by. Filthy in appearance, her hair in tangles, and her britches were more holes than material. Pearl was thin as a rail, and God forgive me for saying so, a bit homely. But with all her faults, little Pearl excelled in personality. People went out of their way to speak to her because no matter how big your troubles, little Pearl's life put your own life back in perspective. As tough as Pearl's life was, she didn't know any better. She accepted it and attacked life with an overwhelming spirit—a spirit people found contagious.

Charity also knew her by the name Prickly Pear. Her father favored the drink, and while waiting outside local taverns, she'd at times fend off drunks with jackknives she kept in her pockets. It was rumored that drunks avoided her because nobody wanted to be poked by the Prickly Pear.

She confounded Charity.

Next morning, watching out the back window, Charity, saw the girl strolling up the path. Quickly grabbing a couple of bags of laundry, she waited on the front porch to start her drama.

"Oh my, oh my, Miss Charity. How you ever gonna' get caught up?" she exclaimed to herself. "I just don't know what you gonna' do to be finished on time," replying to her own question. Watching out of the corner of her eye she saw that all her drama had brought a smile to that little face.

Looking up, "Hello there, child," she kindly said.

"Hello," was the response back.

"Who ya talkin' to?" she asked.

"Why I's just talkin' to the only smart person round here till you come along." Tickled by the comment they both stood sniggering until their eyes watered.

Miss Charity's shack. Drawn by Olivia years later.

"Why, I think I know you girl. You must be Miss LaRaela, don't the folks round town call you Pearl," Miss Charity asked.

"How you know my name?" she asked, wondering if this old woman could read minds.

"Why, we both know some of the same people. The Vicars an old friend to Miss Charity, and he done told me all about you. He thinks you purdy special girl," Charity replied.

"How come you so far behind in your work that you need be frettin' and carryin' on?" she asked.

"I got to do all the laundry for Mr. Orman today, and I got no help," Charity replied, shaking her head in despair.

9

"You don't got to be worried. I'll help you," and with that Miss LaRaela walked over and grabbed hold of a canvas bag of dirty clothes. "Lead the way, Miss Charity."

When the work was well in hand, they sat on the porch of Charity's shack, passing the time of day. Miss Pearl sat gawking in amazement when Charity pulled a fancy pipe from her apron. The bowl was Meerschaum and carved with an exceptionally detailed face of an exotic woman. Charity continued speaking as she packed the bowl of the pipe, struck a match, and began puffing. Pearl never seen, "no woman smokin' no pipe before." Noticing Pearl's amazement, she explained. "My youngest boy, Milton, he up in Tennessee right now. Our master, Mr. Orman, my boy's father, sent him up with his white son, Mr. William Thomas Orman, to help look after and take care a him as long as the war lasts. Mr. William, he write about Milton in a letter, where Mr. William say Milton doin' good and rollin' in the fat, and I pray ever' day Milton still rollin' in that fat."

"I'll pray he is still well off too," Pearl said, wondering herself how the war was going in far-away places.

"That why I smoke this pipe," Miss Charity told her. "It belong to Mr. William Orman. It was his pipe 'til the lady's nose got half broke off, and he don't want it no more. My boy, Milton, tell Mr. William how his mama like smokin' a pipe, so he get that pipe and give it to me as a gift. I smoke it 'cause it remind me of my son Milton."

Charity had told Miss Sadie in the big house what was goin' on, asking, "If it be alright, I try and help the child." And of course, Miss Sadie's gave her full support. Miss Pearl was enamored by the mere presence of Miss Sadie, from the time she first laid eyes on her coming round the house but especially when Miss Sadie gifted her with a couple of her old dresses she had outgrown.

10

After the presentation, Miss Charity began her mission to makin' Miss Pearl more presentable, starting with her rather strong woodsy odor, nothing a long-overdue bath couldn't rectify. There was a bit of a battle getting her in the water and combing out those tangles was a painful struggle, but the final result was viewed by all in a favorable light. Miss Sadie was so taken with the changes in Miss Pearl that she rearranged Charity's duties to allow her more time to help the child. Miss Sadie also enjoyed all the gossip Pearl had picked up around town. Pearl not knowing what gossip was, held nothing back.

It was in the parlor of the Orman House on her first visit where Miss Charity, who remained standing, listened in while Pearl sat on the sofa and visited with Miss Sadie and her mother, Miss Anna. During the conversation, Miss Anna accused Miss Sadie of encouraging gossip and told her to quit being so incorrigible. Miss Anna became frustrated when Miss Sadie continued to ask Pearl about the goings-on in town, prying deeper into the affairs of others. Miss Anna left shaking her head, preferring to sew in the next room, and it was from here she occasionally chuckled and made comments.

Back on Miss Charity's porch in her fine new dress, Pearl asked, "Miss Charity, you done told me about your son Matthew, and I's real sad about Mark diein' and all.... John Milton bein' off to war got to be a terrible burden on the mind, and I'll start prayin' right along with ya, but how 'bout your boy Luke? Tell me a little 'bout Luke."

With a deep sadness, Charity responded, "Oh, the Lord know I has trouble when it come to thinkin' 'bout Luke. He be a most handsome boy, and he be his momma's boy. He were like you in many ways; sharp as a whip he was, never thinkin' 'bout his self, always others. He had a little birthmark, a darker black fish hook under his right eye. It one of the thing 'bout him Mr. Orman put down on paper to help find him ifin' he ever run away. Ain't that somethin', makin' record of people like they was livestock. Why I even knowed lot who was brung back and branded cause they try and run away. Being a good and handsome boy what end up sendin' my Luke away. Mr. Orman, he get an offer to buy Luke from a man who need a houseboy. He'd never sold Luke exceptin' it be one them hard times when the bank putin' the grip on him to pay up on the money he owed. I 'member bein' held back, outa my mind watchin' my little 'un rode off. Nothin' I could do 'bout it. Those holding me back was my friends, I don't hold nothin' again um. They just tryin' to keep me out of trouble, and they all come together after to comfort me. Miss Pearl, I tell you it hurt me even today just thinkin' about my boy. Ain't a day go by he not on my mind."

.....

The next morning Charity woke to a scratching sound. Looking out a window, she discovered Pearl meandering by, dragging a stick and making designs on the dirt path. Always going out of her way to pass unnoticed, today she was intentionally making a noise, as if wanting to be discovered, and by the looks of the path, she had been scratching for some time. If she was hoping for an invitation, she would not be disappointed. Charity appeared in the window. "Mornin', Miss LaRaela."

"Mornin', Miss Charity."

"Miss Pearl, I's just getting ready for some eggs and grits. I don't suppose you might join me; I sure would be grateful for the company. I gets lonely bein' by myself all the time.

"Why, they ain't nothin' I'd rather be doin Miss Charity." Pearl responded, grinning ear to ear. Hurrying into the shack, she was anxious to help.

As they prepared the meal, Miss Charity asked, "Miss Pearl, I don't know much 'bout you. Why don't you talk a spell and tell me 'bout yourself, I be curious as a cat to where you be stayin'. 'Causin' you come in from da swamp back of the house?"

"Oh, I got me a nice place to stay on the *Albany*. Father and I always stay on the *Albany* when he comes to work the cotton season," Pearl responded."

Charity knew the *Albany* and often passed by the old steamer when she'd go into the wetlands collecting herbs and root for her medicines. She remembered the *Albany* from the hurricane of fifty-two, and how when attempting to escape the storm, the *Albany* made a desperate run-up river. Blown off course, the big side-wheeler ran aground on Scipio Creek just north of town. Her hull was ripped apart by the knees of the great cypress trees. She was beyond salvage. With her boiler and hardware long since removed, the derelict steamer lay quietly rotting along the bank of the wetlands. Yes, Charity knew the *Albany* and did not consider it a fit place to live, but she found inspiration in the small child who, knowing no better, viewed it as a palace.

Albany

13

Pearl went on for hours talking about her memories and travels and the people she had met along the way. She opened up about how when she was young, "Be'uns that my mother died and father was always away," she was raised by slave women nurtured by and suckled at the breasts of plantation midwives. Charity thanked God for the instincts of her black sisters, for in their eyes, Pearl was not white but only a child. These midwives believed as was written in Mathew 18:3:

"Unless you are converted and become as little children, you will by no means enter the kingdom of heaven."

Innocent and with a clean soul she was cared for without judgment until she reached an age of accountability when she'd choose her own path.

Pearl started to tear up when she spoke of her Miss Millie, and Miss Millie's husband Ponder, both slaves on the Milton Plantation. She spoke with such kindness that if a person listening didn't know any better, they'd have thought Miss Millie and Ponder were her mother and father. She also mentioned her mother, Ariana, who died in childbirth giving her life, and how it was her fault her mother was dead. "Hold on child, who toll you dat you kill your mother?" Charity asked, with a concerned look.

"My father said it's 'cause a me she's dead, and I don't think he likes me all that much cause of her diein'."

"It ain't your fault you mother die, Miss Pearl."

Interrupting, Pearl accused, "You must have be talkin' to the Vicar 'causin' that's what he says."

"You listen to me girl, Vicar don't got to tell Miss Charity nothin' causin' it the Bible, and it be God hisself that say you ain't to blame. Child is born innocent of sin and not to be held to blame fer nothin'. You father wrong to say you guilty of murderin' your mother. That a burden you don't need be carryin'. Maybe I need have a talk with him. What your father name, Miss Pearl?"

14

"Well, I know it don't make good sense cause my name is LaRaela Retsyo Agnusdei, and his name is Guillaume Gauthier Verheist. But he wouldn't give his name cause he's ashamed of me, and that's why sometimes he calls me his bastard child." Pearl recalled her father's words, scalding like a hot iron when drunken he cursed and cried out, "You may be white, but you always gonna be a no-good nigger for killin' your maw." His words seared into the child's mind, becoming a truth—a hard row to hoe for a child of four. Pearl could not understand the hate in his words because she knew many Negros. They were her family, and she knew none that were, "No good."

"Girl, you quit believin' dis way or I's goin' wash you mouth out with soap for speakin' these lies. You need to trust Miss Charity causin' I's old and wise. You ain't never been no bastard, and you had nothin' to do with your mother's death. You understand me, Miss Pearl." And with that, she gave Pearl a stern look to drive the point home.

"Well, I guess if that's the way God feels 'bout it, I'll have ta change my thinkin'. I won't be sayin' it no more, Miss Charity," Pearl said with a smile. "But you best not tell my father he's wrong. He don't like it when people tell him he's wrong; he might go and hurt someone."

Charity made some inquires around town concerning Pearl's father, and she later related to Miss Sadie, "There be slaves live here from the old times. These slaves, they do not know this man, but they know of his father and his grandfather 'cause they be slavers of the worst kind. I don't believe that apple fall far from that tree 'cause he don't even share his name with Miss Pearl. She carries her mama's name," Miss Charity said. "Pearl's father wanted nothing to do with her and tolerate her because of an oath forced on him by her diein' mother, and I tell you, Miss Sadie, it were a oath to raise the dead again' him ifin' anything happen to her precious Pearl. Bein' he ain't Christian and believe in them dark ways, it what holdin' him at bay when in come to Pearl. Long as he believe, our Pearl be safe."

Not even Miss Charity could identify the face of Pearl's father. She knew from a letter Pearl stored in the wardrobe that he was Belgian, and his name was Guillaume Gauthier Verheist, and the word around town described him as a violent man.

Time passed; the Cotton Season was in full swing, and an old slave woman and a young girl became close friends. It gave Miss Charity a warm feeling in her heart to have a young girl to tend to once again. But being a slave, she knew her ability to help was limited. Growing old as a slave, and becoming useless weight hung heavy on her mind, and she worked herself ragged, worried she might be put out or sold. The Vicar eased her mind some when he arranged for Pearl to help the widow Caroline at the Florida Boarding House. She knew Caroline was a fine upstanding, God-fearing woman, and she thought, *She'll make a fine mother for my fledglin', somthin' happen to me.*

To keep her coming back, Miss Charity encouraged Pearl keep what Pearl called her treasures—included the dresses Miss Sadie's gave here—in a large wardrobe in the front room of her shack, telling Pearl, "You jest come on in here in the mornin' an you can dress so's you look proper when you workin' for Miss Caroline."

As time passed, trust grew, and with invitations to stay with Miss Charity or Miss Caroline, Pearl, no longer wanted to spend her nights alone on the old steamer, especially knowing her father would be gone for weeks gambling and womanizing. Then on a bright, hot June day, Pearl and her father were gone, and those whose lives she had touched were heartbroken. The cotton season was over for the year, and Pearl's father headed North into Georgia to find work on the plantations in the offseason. Heartbroken Miss Charity and Miss Caroline comforted each other, biding their time, knowing she would soon return. In the meantime, conversations with Miss Caroline were of how they might get Pearl away from her father and give the child a more stable life. But Miss Caroline had checked with a solicitor and no judge was ever going to take a daughter away from her father.

Both Charity and Caroline believed it might have been for the best that Pearl was farther inland when on December 18, 1861, the citizens of Apalachicola received disturbing news. The USS Hatteras was now lying just off St. Vincent Island near the site of the dismantled battery. The few Confederate soldiers who remained on the islands reported that a small complement of Union soldiers had visited the abandoned battery on St. Vincent Island and the lighthouse at Cape St. George. Although the Confederates had earlier dismantled and removed the light, it was from this high point that the Union soldiers observed the town. Shortly after the Union returned to their ship, the Confederates slipped in and burned the interior staircase, leaving a hollow shell. The last remnants of the Confederate forces abandoned Apalachicola the week of March 16, 1862, and disappeared into the interior and along the coastline. The people remaining in Apalachicola, realized they were alone and at the mercy of the Union ships. Other than a couple of dozen white families of mostly women and children, a few Italian and Greek oystermen, and a handful of slaves remained, by the week of March 23, 1862; the town had been abandoned.

They were commanded to blockade the port, not occupy the town, but when they did make their presence known, it was in full splendor. In the early morning of Monday, March 24, 1862, citizens realized their greatest fear. Two boats, a cutter, and a whaler launched from the *USS Mercedita.* They carried on board a full complement of heavily armed troops and were rowing toward our town.

17

From sheltered positions, townspeople watched as the boats approached. The whaleboat led the cutter by five-hundred yards, searching the shoreline for signs of aggression. The larger cutter lay waiting, ready to come to the aid of the smaller boat. Both boats approached under a flag of truce. Eventually, both boats came within one hundred yards of the lower wharf and anchored. The oars were kept up, as a signal that the boat commander wished to communicate with Apalachicola leaders.

One half hour passed, and no one from the town came forward. The commander of the Union expedition raised anchor and proceeded toward the lower wharf. The citizens were relieved to see Mayor Anson Hancock and three of our city leaders, City Clerk Sam Benezet, Mr. Richard Gibbs Porter, and John Miller, all prominent merchants, filing onto the dock.

The ranking Union officer introduced himself as Lieutenant Trevett Abbot of the *Mercedita* and reported the object of his mission. Mr. Hancock informed Lieutenant Abbott that by order of the Confederate government the local Confederate command had removed troops, arms, and ammunition the previous week, and he could not speak to their current disposition. He informed Lieutenant Abbott that all inhabitants except for themselves and a few women and children had left.

"We, the few, have remained behind to protect our own properties from incineration threatened from onshore," he said.

Hancock also informed Lieutenant Abbott that the city leaders and the women and children gathered had no authority to represent the new Confederate government.

A perceptive man, Lieutenant Abbott noticed that except for these four leaders, all other citizens watching stayed back a considerable distance. He also noted their nervous demeanor, concluding that some of these men were under threat from Confederate ruffians, so-called Confederates which were now standing in the shadows, watching the proceedings.

He appeared convinced that the same leaders he spoke with were possibly rank secessionists, and that through them, he would never be able to ascertain the true sentiments of the town. Lieutenant Abbott wisely decided not to raise the Union flag or insist that the citizens take the loyalty oath.

He realized that the citizens of Apalachicola were under the threat of death if caught collaborating with the enemy. He concluded the interview and returned to his ship. The citizens of Apalachicola breathed a sigh of relief as he rowed away.

On April 3, 1862, Lieutenant in Command A. J. Drake, of the US gunboat *Sagamore,* launched eight armed boats and captured without resistance the city of Apalachicola, along with all vessels in the vicinity. This was a blow to Southern pride but was viewed as a mixed blessing. At least now, the people no longer had to live with the uncertainty of whether the Federals or the Confederates were in charge of our town.

The people remaining in Apalachicola, mostly women and children, crowded the wharves to watch the eight, heavily-armed boats, landing on our shore.

They earlier had been convinced that the Yankee forces were ruthless Hessians bent on burning, pillaging, and destroying. Because of Lieutenant Abbott, they stood without any fear of mistreatment and seemed to believe that the Yankees might possess a degree of humanity and discipline.

The Yankees once again returned to their ships under command to blockade the port, not occupy the town. Over the course of the war, and much to the disdain of citizenry, the Union returned many times to commandeer supplies and collect intelligence, but the town, for now, did not face the utter destruction previously predicted.

The Union Navy would have been lucky to find four-hundred souls remaining in the entire area. By August 1862, the Union blockaders became very efficient, and under the objections of local leaders, the Confederate army blockaded the last channel that supplied provisions from the North. Many in the town began to suffer from malnutrition.

Apalachicola citizens felt betrayed by the Confederate commanders' decision to cut the last supply line. They looked to the Union blockaders, and the Union responded. Once again, Union boats returned to town and in tow brought several boats that they had captured attempting to run the blockade. The boats presented to the townspeople were to be used to harvest seafood to feed the town.

The gift of the boats came with a warning. If found to be collecting more food than was necessary, the Union would fire on the boats. The health of the town soon improved with a variety of seafood.

Upon her return, Pearl spent most of the 1862 cotton season staying with Miss Caroline and Miss Sadie. Her father had fallen in with a group of ruffians calling themselves the Rebel Guard and was gone most of the time. I have trouble comprehending how some men lack conscience. In the War of Southern Independence, these ruffians plundered and pillaged wherever they went. Under the guise of patriotism, they preyed upon citizens who remained behind. Her father's absence was fine with everyone concerned. Miss Charity, who never wished harm on any of God's creatures, secretly hoped he'd not return.

Distance protected Apalachicola from the carnage of battle. Offshore, we were at the mercy of an impenetrable Union blockade. A small Confederate force still controlled the river to the north, with reconnoiters to Apalachicola recording the movements of the Union Navy. Those citizens remaining in Apalachicola walked a fine line, falling under the scrutiny of the Union blockade offshore and the Confederacy up the river, but the real perceived threat came from neither. The threat that shadowed the town still came from the group of ruffians calling themselves the Rebel Guard. Reports of piracy and death followed in the wake of their movements across the Florida

Panhandle; the most violent of the faction was headed by Pearl's father.

Perhaps the Union presence offshore was the deterrent that up to now had kept them at bay, but this presence was undergoing a change that could inflame the Rebel Guard and draw them downriver to Apalachicola. Over the last few months, most of the white blockade regiments found themselves reassigned north and replaced with, United States Colored Troops—U.S.C.T. regiments.

Adding insult to injury, plantation masters now found themselves held hostage by the very slaves who once worked their lands. Free Northern blacks and runaway slaves would soon make up a large percentage of blockade regiments. In the eyes of a white Union seaman, blockading Florida ports was one of the more boring duties of the war. Still, white Union sailors sought these positions because bounty taken from captured blockade vessels went to auction. Portions of profits were divvied up among the crew according to rank, making it a boring but profitable duty.

Excited, because when the time came, she had been chosen by the Trinity ladies to place the baby Jesus in the crib, Pearl eagerly shared her news with Miss Charity, who to her surprise seemed skeptical at best, concerning this new Christmas holiday. Charity, questioned if it was even Christian, muttering aloud, "Celibratin' Jesus birthday, ain't one thing in the Bible 'bout it, and I knowed causin' I knowed the good book, cover to cover." She loved the story of the birth as much as anybody but struggled with the fact they didn't celebrate, "no special day in da Bible. Why dey don't know fer sure the day he born?" Looking back, she remembered it wasn't until the mid-1850s that some Southern families started having get-togethers on December 25[th.] Just adopting a random day to celebrate the birth of her Christ didn't seem quite right to her.

"It was them Germans that started the season down the wrong path. Who ever heard of bringing a tree into the house? What that got to with anythin', and now shops downtown was startin' selling expensive bobbles made of glass for decoration, as if spending all that money made peoples more Christian. Then to top that off, they stuck that tree right in the front window to put they Christianity on parade. Nothing Christian about dat," she muttered.

But when it came right down to it, she had to admit, the season was startin' to grow on her. It was more important than ever to find any reason to hold people together especially now with the threat of this terrible war looming on the horizon. She felt she had gotten her point across when out of nowhere, Pearl told her, "I believe that Jesus views slaves much as that old widow in the story. You know, when she dropped two copper coins in the collection box. Jesus was tellin' his disciples all 'bout her 'cause although she's poor, she give all she had. Why, my black family is closer to God in a shack with a dirt floor than any white master in a grand manor house. Most ain't able to read, but quote long scriptures from memory; it's 'cause they carry the words in their hearts."

Miss Charity now sat humbled before a child who found no value in worldly possessions, instead finding great treasure in the search for understanding. Taking Pearl in her arms, she assured her, "Oh you blessed child. I know God got a special purpose for your life. God is all knowin' and do things in his own time and in his own way, and he ain't ready to tell you your purpose yet. But when God ready, you'll know, and Miss Charity can't think of nobody better than you to carry out his will. Miss Pearl, I want you to 'member, I'll always be here to help you anyway I can." Miss Charity gave Pearl hope, and it was in that moment that Pearl began searching her mind for a gift, a wonderful gift, a gift grand enough to thank her for all her kindness.

Helping to mend Pearl's life became Charity's purpose, but noticing the changes, Pearl's father didn't take kindly to an, "Old nigger woman's meddling." He stated to one of his Rebel Guards, "She'll pay."

******

A few days passed, and Miss Charity traveled the path along the shoreline returning home. Her basket contained the few provisions she procured to sustain the Orman family. She occasionally glanced at the impressive row of cotton warehouses off to her left. Seeing a white man approaching, she stepped off the trail onto the water's edge, and standing silent with her eyes down she yielded the path. Without warning he violently turned and shoved her into the shallow water. Without hesitation, he rushed forward following her down and began kicking her savagely. He gave blow after blow to her back then rolling her over he gave her two blows to the stomach.

The few slaves still working the wharf knew Miss Charity but could do nothing. It wasn't until one of the warehouse owners took notice; he knew Thomas Orman and recognized the slave woman he had sent to help care for his ailing wife. Looking over to his men he pointed yelling, "For God's sake, help her!"

The assailant seeing the men rushing toward him pointed a defiant finger at Miss Charity, threatening, "That girl is mine. Quit puttin' them thoughts in her head." As he ran away down the shoreline he hollered back, "Next time I'll kill ya!"

Miss Charity was in a bad way. A couple of the men gently lifted her, carrying her to a wagon, and they were ordered to take her home. Upon hearing the news, Thomas Orman was furious, and he sent men out looking for the assailant. Miss Sadie sent for Dr. Chapman and rushed to Miss Charity's side to offer aid. "Who did this to you?" Sadie ordered.

In great distress, Miss Charity whispered, "It be Pearl's father, but please, Miss Sadie, don't tell Pearl." Gripping Sadie's arm, she repeated, "Pearl, can't never know." Then once again she pleaded, "Please Miss Sadie promise me you don't tell Pearl." With nothing left, she succumbed to the pain, closing her eyes.

Dr. Chapman did what he could, but as always, his final prognosis, "Give her time to heal. It's in God's hands now... We've no choice but to wait and see." She had a bad bruise over her right kidney and several fractured ribs. Dr. Chapman bound her ribs, giving her laudanum for the pain, but told Miss Sadie everything depended on if she's bleeding internally. He told Sadie, "I wish I had the ability, to see inside, but even knowing the damage to her liver and kidney, there's not much that could be done." To prepare Sadie for the worst, he added, "Miss Orman, keep in mind she's very old. There's only so much you can do at this point; keep her quiet, and I'll check back tomorrow." Over time, Miss Charity's kindness had touched many. As word of the assault spread, the prayers added up quickly.

Miss Sadie stayed by her side through the night. At times, Charity became so quiet Sadie held a mirror to her mouth praying for one more breath. Pearl arrived at the crack of dawn; Sadie, waiting on the porch, signaled for her to sit. "Miss Pearl, we need to sit and have a talk because Miss Charity is feeling poorly this morning."

"What's wrong with her, Miss Sadie," Pearl inquired.

"Well... you know Miss Charity is getting up there in age, and sometimes older people suffer from what Miss Charity always called the decrepitude," Sadie explained.

"What is that?" Pearl asked.

"It's a little hard to explain because it sometimes is not just one thing but a lot of little things that go wrong and pile up as you get old. Now... I'm hoping you might be able to help Miss

24

Charity recover by helping me care for her. Would you be able to help me take care of her?" From the very start of the conversation, the look of concern on Pearl's face assured Miss Sadie of two certainties. She'd not be alone caring for Charity, and she was no longer in charge.

Pearl did not leave Charity's side except to fetch needed items from the big house. She insisted on staying in the room during Dr. Chapman's follow up visits and was not fooled when they whispered, talking in circles around the facts. It was obvious to Pearl, Charity was not just sick but injured. It was just before Charity's bout with this so-called decrepitude that Pearl's father had threatened, telling her, "You askin' too many questions, Pearl. You need to learn to keep your mouth shut. Bad things can happen to a child and her friends if'n she talks too much." The look he gave her sent chills down the center of her back.

Pearl was torn with guilt because nowadays, anytime bad things happened, she inevitably suspected her father. But now she felt sure, and Miss Charity was the last straw. She'd no longer give her father the benefit of the doubt, and she plainly saw his hand all over this attack.

After a few days, Charity was able to sit up and take nourishment on her own. With Miss Sadie's assurance, Pearl felt it safe to leave Miss Sadie in charge and spend some time helping Miss Caroline down at the boarding house. Little did Pearl know when she started for Miss Caroline's, the fruitful day that lie ahead. Approaching City Square, she noticed people hurrying toward the wharf. Asking passerbys, "What's goin' on?"

With an irritated expression, and no sign of slowing a man responded. "It's the blockaders; they done brought a bunch of them nigger soldiers into town askin' questions 'bout somethin'. We on the way to findin' out what," and he hurried on.

25

Unnoticed, Pearl scowled at the man and his obvious hatred of all black people; people that she felt he didn't even know. Down at the docks stood an impressive row of finely dressed United States Colored Troops—some of the best of the U.S.C.T. regiment that now manned the ships blockading the passes.

Pearl was excited to see so many black faces dressed in all their finery, lined up on display for all the see, it was an impressive sight indeed. She saw pride in the faces of free black soldiers standing there, choosing to take control by ignoring the few who jeered. Pearl stood facing the soldiers behind their commander, following along just behind him and in front of the crowd as he slowly inspected his troops. She'd seen this before, it was a show of force, reminding people they were in charge. She was especially taken by one soldier whose uniform carried a large number of bars and decoration. In addition to a rife, he carried a sword on a gold sash.

She could tell they were about to receive the return to ship order. Suddenly she noticed something very special about the soldier with the sword. It was the most perfect little, dark black, fish hook marking under his right eye. Pearl gasped in disbelief. "*Is this even possible?*" she asked herself. She had to know for sure, so when the twenty men turned walking toward their boat, Pearl yelled out, "Luke," and only one man, her soldier, looked back. Pearl held in her excitement but was ready to burst. She'd just found Charity's special Christmas gift, and it was a gift beyond her wildest dreams. Pearl was going to give Miss Charity her son.

Pearl didn't know if she was coming or going. Her mind was buzzing like a beehive. One thing she knew for sure was she had to talk to that soldier, and she also knew it wasn't going to be easy getting out to the blockade. She was going to need some help, and she knew just who to ask, Captain Hatch Wefing.

For quite some time Pearl had been working on a plan to try and assemble a family from spare parts, and by parts, she meant those people who seemed lost and needed a family. There was a time she'd felt Captain Hatch Wefing would be the perfect father and Miss Caroline the perfect mother. But Miss Caroline's reaction was anything but encouraging, remembering back to when she had mentioned his name as a suitor.

Miss Caroline, evidently not only knew of Captain Hatch Wefing but had grown up under the power of his charm. In her best stage voice, she dramatically stated, "Alack and alas, it was simply not to be, for my Captain had a wandering eye." This was followed by a good laugh by all at the table. He had a good heart but his wandering eye had stood in the way of romance, so for now, he'd be relegated to the position of uncle.

Captain Hatch was always one step ahead of those who might accuse him of being a profiteer. He had connections both north and south. Secretly loved by the ladies, and admired by men, he was often criticized for his socially festive ways catering to aristocrats and slaves alike. By far the best choice for a covert undertaking.

Upon presenting Hatch with her plan he made it plain. "Girl you're goin' owe me big time; this is going to cost me some very good cigars and a couple of bottles my best bourbon. She knew he lived for this kind of thing, and no matter what he said, he was all in. He said, "How about tomorrow night you meet me down at the docks just after dark, and you got to promise me, not to tell a soul." Pearl complied assuring him of her silence.

Next night, just offshore, Captain Hatch raised the sail on the small skiff heading toward the blockade. With a half-mile to go, he lit a lantern and began singing a song that contained rather questionable lyrics. He told Pearl, "Don't you worry none; I'm just announcing our visit." It should have come as no surprise that the men on board knew exactly who was coming and went out of their way to bring him onboard. It was the same reaction he'd have received from a visit to Confederate Command.

While Hatch did a little trading keeping the command occupied, filling whiskey glasses, and lighting cigars, Pearl wandered out on deck, striking up a conversation with one of the colored troopers. "Where ya from?" she asked.

"I hail from New York, young Miss," he replied.

"I've heard of New York and even seen a few pictures of that big city you got up there. You ever been to that big city?" she asked.

"Why, yes Miss, that be the part of New York I'm from," he replied, with a slight smile, thinking of home.

"You wouldn't happen to know Luke would ya? I seen him in town last time you was there. He's got a gold sash and carries a sword if that helps."

"Why yes I know Luke," and before he could finish his thought the door behind him opened, and there stood the man himself, the man she hoped to be Luke. He had been sitting at a small table beneath the window writing a letter, and he couldn't help but overhear the conversation outside.

"Last time I's in town, I heard a young girl holler my name. Could that have been you by chance?" he asked.

"Yes sir, that was me alright."

"How is it you seem to know me, but I don't recall you?" he inquired.

"Well, to be honest, I ain't yet sure I do know you, but if that little black fishhook under your right eye is the birthmark, I think it is, I still may not know you but I do know your mama," she said with a smile."

He stood there stunned, unable to utter a single word.

Pearl told him, "If you think for a second you might a been born down here, and you recollect your mama's name bein' Charity, we need to have ourselves a talk."

Shaking his head in disbelief, "This doesn't seem possible you being here, and speaking these things to me. I volunteered for duty guarding this pass because I had a feeling about this place. There was something about the name of the town... It somehow felt familiar to me. I know this name Charity, but over the past few years, I was beginning to feel I may have heard it in a dream... that it wasn't real. But here you are telling me you know my mama, and her name is Charity. Please tell me I'm not dreaming and you are real."

"Luke, I'm Pearl, and I'm real as can be. You don't know it yet, but your 'bout to become the best, most special gift I could ever imagine givin'. If it'd be alright with you, I'd like to get the two of you together for a long overdue visit."

"Well I have to tell you; I never expected such big news to arrive in such a small package," said Luke.

"You'll need to remember the man who brought me, his name is Captain Hatch Wefing, and you can trust him. I'll send word with Captain Hatch as soon as I can arrange things," Pearl told him.

Why don't I just come in with an escort and visit mama? Seems like it'd be simpler," Luke suggested."

Pearl reasoned with Luke. "The way I figure it, the fewer to known the better. If the locals found out her son was a soldier with the Union blockade, they's some might accuse her of bein' a spy, and we don't want that to happen," Pearl explained.

In the brief time she had left, she told Luke about his brothers Mathew, Mark, and John Milton. Telling him if he gets up around Bragg's army, "To watch out for John Milton cause he's travelin' with his white half-brother, William T. Orman, in the war. Luke, Miss Charity is very special to me," but that's all she could say before the love got stuck in her throat, and the tears started flowing.

Seeing the love in Pearl's eyes, Luke tried to ease the moment, "Pearl I can see you love my mother deeply, and the way I look at it, I think it kinda makes you my sister. What I mean to say is, anybody go to the all the trouble you have to find me, well... I'd be proud to call you my sister, if that be okay with you Pearl?"

Sniffling, trying desperately to hide the tears, Pearl embraced her new brother, and with that hug, Luke and the solider watching started tearing up. Of course with his perfect timing, and in that exact moment, Captain Hatch stuck his head in the door, took one look, and exclaimed, "Pearl... what in the world is goin' on? What did you say to them? Oh, don't tell me, I already know. This has got to be Luke. Don't feel bad for crying, Luke. After meetin' Pearl, for one reason or another, in the end, we all find a reason to shed a tear." After a short chuckle, we said our goodbyes and sailed for home.

It took time to tack in against the wind and it was near two a.m. before they arrived back. Pearl snuck into Miss Charity's shack and fell asleep, sitting in a chair with her head on the table. Now that Miss Charity was getting back up and around, she had plans to keep her in sight both day and night to make sure whatever happened didn't happen again. When Charity rose, Pearl had the table set with cheese, bread, and honey. Miss Charity said it was perfect but went ahead and fried a couple of eggs with bacon to complete the menu.

Charity felt Pearl's time better spent down helping Miss Caroline at the boarding house restaurant instead of, "Followin' me around all day," she told her.

But Pearl insisted she needed to come along to keep her safe, till they found Orman's slave Big Henry sitting on the porch. "Mornin', Miss Charity. Hopin' I did't startle you none," Henry apologized.

"Not a'tall, Henry. What is it I can do fer you?" Charity asked.

"Well, it ain't what you do fer me, but what I do fer you. See Mr. Tom and Miss Sadie thinin' it be best I kinda stay with you fer a while and hep you get around and haul da things you find. Now, I knowed what you gona say, and da fact is, they's my orders, and I thinkin' they's purdy good orders dat I's goin' follow ifin' it's to ur likin' or not."

Pointing her finger right at him she says, "Well in dat case I 'pose you best come along, but don't you be slowin' me down none. You has to keep up. It look bad fer you ifin' you can't keep up with old Miss Charity.

"I do the best I can, Miss Charity," he said with a smile.

"Pearl, you just as well go help Miss Caroline; I suspect she could use some help 'bout right now."

31

"I suspect your right. Henry, you take good care Miss Charity, ya hear," Pearl ordered.

"Oh, I will, Miss Pearl; I will," Henry assured her.

Pearl had a stop to make before heading on to the Florida Boarding House. With only a week before Christmas, she needed to find her Captain Hatch and make arrangements for Luke's homecoming. She found him down at the docks, laughing and sharing a small libation with some of the slaves. Apparently, he believed a hair of dog might brace him to face a new day after a night of debauchery "Uncle Hatch we need to make plans," she stated.

"Now Pearl, don't you be frettin' none 'cause your old Uncle Hatch has already got it all worked out," he replied in a loud and somewhat inebriated tone.

"Keep your voice down," she scolded.

"You just pick the time, and I'll be seen passing town with a slave going out fishing. When I return, I'll pass by town with a slave on board, and no one but you and me need know it ain't the same slave," he said, looking over to the other slaves shushing them to secrecy with his finger to his lips.

"Pearl had to admit, even inebriated, it sounded like a good plan. "Have him at Miss Charity's the evening of the 24th," Pearl commanded.

"You can count on me, Miss Pearl. Old Uncle Hatch has the situation under control, Miss Pearl, Yes mam, Miss Pearl." He assured her, giving a small salute, Pearl shook her head over his intoxication while the slave gave a little chuckle.

The 24th arrived, and Pearl was beside herself. Miss Charity suspected nothing and was working hard to convince Pearl to spend her first real Christmas Eve with Miss Sadie or Miss Caroline and to be sure to attend the special service planned down to the Trinity. Miss Charity said assuring Pearl, "Don't you be worryin' 'bout me. I toll you how I fell 'bout celebratin' Christmas. Like always, I be just fine sitting with a little hot cider with the good book keepin' me company. I's fine, feelin' good as ever. You just go and have yourself a good time."

Miss Charity was working in the big house, when good to his word, her Captain tie up to Orman's dock. She hardly recognized Luke in old work clothes. Keeping a wary eye, she hurried him into Charity's shack. Offering him some fresh milk and cheese, the unlikely pair waited there in anticipation.

Long about twilight, Miss Charity came out the back door of the big house heading home. She stopped briefly, surprised to see a lantern light shining out her window. Pearl greeted her at the door leading her inside. She took notice of the man in the room and ask Pearl, "Now... what you up to girl, and who is this fine lookin' gentleman you got sittin' at my table? Sitting her down in the chair across from Luke, Charity, strained to see his face in the dimming light.

"I got you a present Miss Charity."

Interrupting, Miss Charity said, "Why Pearl, you know I already got Henry to walk around and keep me safe. What you got this man talked into?"

"It'd be best to let him explain," Pearl replied, grinning ear to ear.

Luke was beside himself looking into the eyes of his mother. Suffering from a lack of words all he could think to do was describe himself.

"It wasn't till I saw this house sitting here on the bluff that the memories started flooded back. I was starting to think my recollection of the day they took me away may of a been something I'd seen in a nightmare. I remember bein' more scared than I'd ever been before. Looking back, seeing my mama held back and wailing so mournful as to wake the dead. They didn't tell me what was going on. For all I knew, I's just goin' for a ride." Suddenly Miss Charity held her hand to her face. "They put me on a steamer, down below, on the lower deck, sleepin' with the livestock. By the time I finally came to rest, I's on a big old plantation way up north of Atlanta were Master Clay was a trainin' me to be his house boy. Up to that day, I didn't know I was a slave, 'cause my mama had raised me to be free."

Overwhelmed, Miss Charity burst out, "Oh, sweet Jesus, it cain't be." Rising from her chair, she turned up the lantern's wick. Her hand trembled as she withdrew a pair of broken spectacles from her skirt pocket. Gently touching Luke's face, with her eyes full of tears, she found her once steady legs now quivered. Her knees buckled, and she dropped toward the floor, praising God for her miracle. Catching her, Luke pulled her onto his lap for a long heartfelt embrace.

It was still not perfectly clear to Pearl why people cry when they're happy, but with tears in her own eyes, she was starting to understand a little better. Pearl preferred, "Talkin' to hugin'," and in her words later to the Vicar said, "It wasn't until after she'd held him and kissed him all over his face that Miss Charity settled back into her chair, allowin' him to finish his story."

"So... go on tellin' your story. You here so I thinkin' you must be free?" Charity puzzled.

"Three years later, after master Clay's heart up and stopped on him, it was his widow, Miss Clara, sold me away to the Holcomb plantation up in the state of Maryland where I became a steward for Judge Holcomb. I was careful to mind my Ps and Qs 'cause he had a terrible temper. Everyone knew he wasn't much of a farmer. He's always quick to whip a field slave tryin' to justify his own short comings.

"I belonged to Judge Holcomb for six years, until the strangest thing happens. It was late one night when this old black woman show's up looking for some of her relations. Now... I had heard stories of this woman, and how she'd been helpin' slaves escape their masters for freedom in the north, but I never thought I'd meet her in person. Miss Tubman told me to come along if I value my freedom, 'cause to her way of thinking, it was better to be dead than a slave. Since I had no ties and always wonder about freedom, I decided to go along with her to find mine. We traveled by night, stayin' hid at the homes of mostly folks of the Quaker religion, a fine bunch of folks that never believed in slavery.

"It was 1851 when I made my way north, but I had no idea how far it would take me. What I didn't know about was this Fugitive Slave Act that President Millard Fillmore had put into law the year before. The United States Congress passed this, Fugitive Slave Act, September 1850. It bein' a part of the Compromise of 1850—compromise worked out between Southern slave-holding interests and Northern Free-Soilers. Among some northers, the Fugitive Slave Act stoked the fear of what was known as the 'slave power conspiracy,' movin' them to support the act out of fear of an uprisin'. The act required all escaped slaves, upon capture, to be returned to their masters. The act also required that officials and citizens of Free States had to assist officials in enforcin' the law. Abolitionists nicknamed it the 'Bloodhound Law' for the dogs they used to track down runaway slaves. Making the law is one thing, enforcin' it is another, especially when big money is involved. The bounty for runaways was high enough for slavers to justify kidnapping. It didn't matter if you was a free black or not, if they could get you out of state, they bound you, sent you south, and sold you into slavery. Some in the north believed in the law, but many did not, and that cause a great divide among the people of the northern states

"So… it was cause of the Fugitive Slave Act, and through what they call the Underground Railroad that I wound up in Canada a free man. I spend the last eight years there, married me a fine woman from North Carolina, and Mama, someday I hope to introduce you to your Granddaughter, Abigail." Pulling a pocket watch from his vest pocket, he showed Charity a picture of his family, although she had trouble seeing through the tears.

Luke continued, "When the war broke out, I figured it was my duty to volunteer and help other men, like me, find they freedom. I volunteered down here in Apalachicola, hoping to liberate the people, and maybe find my family, and hard as it is to believe, 'cause of Pearl, here I am, sittin' here, in my birthplace, talkin' to my Mama".

Listening intently, only sometimes looking down to stroke Abigail's picture in the cover of the pocket watch, Miss Charity was filled with pride, telling Luke, "Ain't Christian to feel this much pride, but I cain't seem to hep it. I's about to explode like a stick o' that dynamite like they makin' upriver."

Luke assured her, "Mama that ain't pride you feeling. What you be feeling is grace, and grace be God's greatest gift to those who serve him well, and I tell you I's surprised you ain't blowed up years ago 'cause a all the grace God be stuffin' in you.

The homecoming was a great success, and Pearl could see how God's hand had led her down the path. After that, Miss Charity never missed an opportunity to stand in the crowd, secretly admiring her son, in his fine uniform, fighting for freedom.

The End

The Decision

SR Staley

"Holly shit, is that real?"

Nicole twisted her nose and lips in a perplexed grimace as Jack pointed out the obvious. The bench outside an attorney's office—or was it a dermatologist?—seemed unusually cold as frost nipped at her exposed cheeks and hands in the fading light. Her knit cap kept her usually straight, shoulder-length brown hair neatly tucked out of sight, except for a few strands escaping into the still air. She sighed. Jack could be really annoying.

"Damn, Nic, you have to be excited!" he prodded, letting his index finger tap a large white envelope, trying to coax her into some kind of reaction.

She ran her hands along the edges of the sealed envelope, checking its thickness for the umpteenth time. *This couldn't be real*, she thought, a numbness slowing her thoughts.

"Why do you have to swear all the time?"

Jack's arm snaked around her back to brace her head as he pressed a kiss to the side of it just above the ear. "Ah, babe, you love it! You know you do."

She shook her head, dislodging his caress. She lifted a palm to wipe a defiant tear which had escaped onto her cheek. "Your father wouldn't be happy if he knew how much you swore."

"Ha!" Jack chortled. "Poppy got his college nickname, 'Rowdy,' for a reason!"

"I've never heard him swear."

Jack cast a cagy eye her way. "That doesn't mean he doesn't do it. He wouldn't want to corrupt the little children."

"Well, my dad would not be happy."

Jack caught the next words before he said them. He nodded. "I don't swear in front of your dad."

"Well it would be nice if you wouldn't swear so much in front of me, either."

"Oh, come on, Nic." Jack's tone was subdued, as if she had wounded him. "You know," he continued but let his voice trail off to silence. He sat for a few more moments beside her on the bench, letting Nicole sit in her thoughts.

Nicole shook her head and sent her fingers around the corners of the envelope again. She let her teeth roll her lower lip. The envelope's thickness foretold a future that should be sending her into ecstasy. The distinctive but varied seven vertical bars—six black, one maroon dot to draw out the "i" and one short horizontal bar at the end to literally cross the "t," outlining M.I.T.—sketched out pathways she couldn't possibly fathom unless she took the next step: accepting the offer, on a full ride. Yet even the elegant logo of the nation's top computer engineering school couldn't overcome the dread that locked her heart.

Dad would be heartbroken. Sure, he would be proud. But she knew more than anyone else how much he was counting on her to follow him into the family business. A fifth generation Klaas. The business was much too big for him to manage by himself. Plus, he needed someone he could trust. Particularly since Mom, his soulmate, died right after her eighth-grade year. Now, Nicole was an adult. She could start taking over the reins. So, he thought.

Jack pulled his arm back from Nicole's neck, leaving his hand on her shoulder as the other pulled her chin toward him. He brushed another tear from her face. Nic directed her eyes down, toward the unopened envelope.

"Shit, you haven't told him, have you?"

Nicole let out a hollow, shuddering gasp as she tried to keep more tears from cascading out from the wells of her eyes. "He's going to be so upset."

"Does he even know you applied?"

Jack leaned back on the bench as Nicole looked at her shoes, one knee shaking as if pumping water from the frozen ground to keep their bench, the wooden sidewalk, and the entire town afloat above the Arctic Ocean.

"He's a dad. He'll want what is best for you. Just like Poppy wants what's best for me."

"Since Mom died—"

"Nic, it's been four years."

"He needs me."

"Babe, he'll make due. Poppy and Ma were thrilled when I got into Johns Hopkins' early decision."

Jack turned his body to sit square on the bench, as if someone had just snapped his brain to attention. He looked out onto Main Street, ignoring the glow from the buildings on the other side of the road. His arms came down to his sides. He slowly shook his head.

"Jesus." The timbre of Jack's voice had turned sharp. "When the hell did you find out?"

Nicole flipped up the envelope as if to say the answer was obvious. "Can't you stop swearing? Maybe it would be easier to talk to you about this stuff. I wouldn't be so distracted."

"I've been swearing as long as we've been dating."

"Yeah, but it's annoying.

Jack sighed. "When did you find out about MIT?"

41

Nicole lifted her gaze, but instead of turning to Jack, she stared out across the darkened crystal-snow swept street. Even though the streets were well lit for the deepest dark of winter, nothing seemed to be in front her except the white frost covering the sidewalk and road. Even the two-story buildings and shops just across the two-lane main street seemed to fade into the darkness. "December 15th."

"The Early Decision deadline? That's the same day I found out about Johns Hopkins! You checked online? I told you about Johns Hopkins. Why didn't you... why didn't you...." Jack's voice trailed off again before saying in a resolute voice: "Nic, you've got to tell your dad."

Nicole looked at Jack, her eyes wide with incredulity. "You know Dad. You and me..., we've been dating since middle school.... You saw what happened when Mom passed. You think I can just bounce in and tell him his dreams of a father-daughter wonder business have just gone up in smoke?"

Jack turned back to Nicole. "Are you going to turn down MIT? I don't think so!"

Jack's shoulders fell. His cheeks and the corners of his mouth relaxed. He lifted a hand to her cheek to wipe away more tears with his thumb. "Sorry, Nic." His eyes began to glisten as he let his forehead connect to hers.

He looked directly into her eyes. "But, Babe, you've got to tell him. You guys need to talk this out."

Jack turned back toward the street as he sank back onto the bench. He swore under his breath. He lifted his knees to his chest as he wrapped his arms around them into a ball as they continued to sit.

"I can't believe it!" he grumbled, shaking his head. "You found out about MIT two weeks ago? And you didn't tell *me*?"

"Just shut up," Nicole murmured, a shallow heave keeping back another sob. "Dad's not ready for this. He's not ready for me to leave the family business." Nicole lifted the forearm of her wool sweater, rubbing her eyes. "Why can't you understand that? You've been in this town as long as I have. You know everybody expects me to join him in the business. You know Dad just assumes I'll do something online rather than leave home for four years."

Jack shifted his weight, freeing his legs, and rolled on a hip to plunge his hand into his pocket and pull out a bandana. "Fuck."

He reached over to Nicole, gently pulled the envelope out of her hand and placed it next to him. He threw a leg over her legs so he could straddle her lap, and looked directly into her tear-streaked face. One of the many benefits of being four feet tall was he could sit just like this, looking into the most beautiful brown eyes he could ever imagine, even though she stood five foot five inches. Three locks of her brown hair crept out from underneath her favorite hat adorned with the seasonal rows of snowflakes and snowmen, giving her a childish youth well below her years. He figured she was partial to his blond locks. And curls. And rugged jawline. Why else would she continue to date him since middle school? Now, however, Jack could see the fear that chased any childlike demeanor away, the culmination of personal turmoil and confusion created by four years of heartbreak.

"Babe," he said, his voice gentle, lifting the cloth to her cheek. "Your dad'll be fine."

Jack leaned toward her, bringing his mouth to hers. He felt the gentle tug of her lips on his as she accepted his kiss. "He'll be fine," he repeated, letting his forehead rest on hers, even though he knew saying it a second time wouldn't help.

Nicole lifted her arms around Jack and pulled him close, her face buried in the insulated shoulder of his bomber jacket.

Jack felt silky strands of her hair brush across his cheeks and fall through his fingers as they embraced. He heard the steady breath of a sigh.

"It's too soon," she whispered.

"Nic, your mom was really sick for years, and she's been gone for four."

"But he'll be all alone. He can't run the business by himself."

Jack laughed. He looked up at the sign of Crump and Crump, LLC, family law. He looked down at her and pulled her lips to his, kissed her again, and rolled smoothly back onto the bench, his arm raised with a flourish. "Look around you!"

Nicole surveyed the street, the sidewalks, the faux wood buildings that lined Main Street, the shops on the first floor, the homes and a few offices above. True enough, the streets were filling as people of average size mingled unremarkably with all manner of dwarfs. The energy of the street was deliberate, relaxed, and much more akin to a small town in the Alaskan bush or the farming towns of prior centuries in the Lower Forty-Eight. Their pace was set by their focus, attending to last minute errands before holing up for dinner and a quiet evening. No meandering today, although truly relaxed traveling was just off the horizon in January. A welcome relief from the craziness of just two days earlier, the day after Christmas.

******

A warmth filled Nicole, drawing any remaining tears back inside. Her father had built this place. He was still building it. Her heart skipped. But was he ready to let her leave it all?

"I guess we need to start heading back," she said, lifting herself up from the bench.

Jack slipped off onto the wood slats knitting together the sidewalk, letting his boots claw into the ice as he seized the acceptance envelope. "I'll walk you home."

Nicole let her hand fall into Jack's, and they edged down the road toward the far side of town and her home. She drew in a breath. The air was crisp, as it always was, and dry. The streets were finally getting back to normal. Christmas was the worst. Everyone was working a full press up to December 26th, even though they were largely done with the heavy lifting of their seasonal work by the 20th. No one, of course, could fully rest easy until January 1st. Still, December 26th was the practical end to everything: Christmas, Hanukkah, Boxing Day, even Kwanzaa—because everything needed to be shipped out. Well, almost everything. Ōmisoka was big, and getting bigger, in Japan. But the Japanese were so well organized and efficient everything they needed was done by the 26th, too.

Still, inevitably, something would crop up before—a logistical foul up, a missed communication with a partner in the Lower Forty-Eight, a software glitch. Who knew what? Five decades of technical effort, the latest in digital technology, and five generations of Klaases couldn't come up with anything more certain than the certainty that something unpredictable would come up and risk fouling up everything.

Not that she and Jack and their families hadn't tried. Even working with Jack's father, the chief software engineer at NP Enterprises, they couldn't come up with the AI code that could predict the next failed cog in the wheel. Their teachers at Florida Virtual School, brilliant and helpful as they were, tried everything. But Jack and Nicole quickly outstripped their expertise and practical knowledge. Working at the North Pole tended to have that effect. Of course, it would have helped if she could have told them about the business, what they were trying to do, and why they were doing it. But she couldn't. Divulging that information risked destroying everything her father, her grandfather, and her great-grandfather—the entire Klaas family line—had built.

Jack's father was brilliant, but they just couldn't figure it out. And the computer science teachers simply couldn't fathom the depth of the problem, let alone envision a solution. They

45

could create simulations that predicted every historical outcome, but they could not predict the next one. The teachers just thought they were making it up. But they weren't. And the stakes were high.

Starting the email relationship with the professor at MIT helped a lot. But even she couldn't help much without knowing more about the details of *The Business*. Their side projects, however, were fun, and Nicole was sure that getting the co-authorship on the research note in an engineering journal sealed her fate on her admissions application. She wondered what the MIT prof would think when she learned she was corresponding with a kid from the North Pole, not Pensacola, Florida.

This year, the problem came from a cold war turning hot when Cambodia reignited tensions with Thailand, jeopardizing the supply chain for an entire distribution group tied to *The Business*. Her father didn't complain—when does Santa Claus ever complain?—and the town, led by Rowdy Hatchet and team, pulled together to get the distribution system back on track.

But, damn, if she could come up with the program, one that learned from itself, real artificial intelligence, and predicted the next bottleneck, screw up, or systems failure, their business would go to entirely new levels. Exponential growth. Nicole smiled at the thought of the breakthrough's effect... for her father, for the town, for millions of kids across the world.

Four years of effort and she still didn't have it. Ugh.

Nicole squeezed Jack's hand.

Jack's snapped a look at her.

"I was just remembering those nights we worked with your pop to get those shoes and clothes out of Thailand," Nicole said.

Jack smirked. "Poppy's been with your father since he took over the North Pole. Being Santa's Number One has its drawbacks. We needed to get that stuff across the Pacific

Ocean... fast! Those were long damn nights, weren't they? But we got the code to work."

"I wasn't so sure," Nicole said. She slipped her hand out of Jack's and pushed it around his shoulders to bring him in closer. They passed Peter Baaker's Pub. She was too tired to stop at the pub. Crying was draining. Jack must have sensed her mood because he didn't break their stride. "I thought I was going to have to rush order a whole new line of shirts from Vietnam."

"That was a pretty intense twenty-four hours, for sure. But man, was it fun!"

They laughed, remembering how Jack's dad had kept feeding them lines of code as they tried to reprogram the master algorithms and then embed protocols to accommodate the unexpected shift orders and queue new suppliers. His mom kept painstaking track of each letter, punctuation mark, and symbol. Their program kept failing, until Jack finally found the comma up against a quotation mark with no space. Once they added the space, voilà!

Jack looked up to Nicole. "You were amazing. I don't think Poppy had ever seen someone process so much in so short a time."

Nicole returned his look. "You were pretty awesome, too. I am not sure we would have made the deadline if you hadn't found that comma. You should think about software programming."

"Nah, I want to give a shot at biomedical engineering," Jack said, but his voice softened as if he had just realized he was talking about a taboo subject.

The next several steps were silent as they peered into windows and re-read signs that they had read thousands of times already.

"Johns Hopkins will be great," Nicole said in a matter of fact tone.

"I just didn't think MIT was the right fit."

"You mean you didn't think I would get in?"

Jack dropped Nicole's hand and stopped cold. "That's not what I meant, Nic."

Nicole sighed. She leaned over and embraced Jack in a hug. "I know, I'm sorry. It's just going to be hard. Being apart. And being away from Dad."

The dread returned as she remembered the last time her father had left her. Weeks passed. She hadn't realized, or was too young to figure out that her parents would never take a week long vacation without her. When they returned, her life became a thick, dark, blur, lacking definition or solace. She felt the beat of her heart heavy in her chest.

Jack kissed Nicole on her cheek before letting her go. "Yeah, but we can still see each other, right? We'll be back at Christmas. We've got a gazillion social media apps we can try."

A smile cracked her solemn mood. "Ha, we should probably just design one!"

They dipped into a darker than usual shadow along the sidewalk. Nicole kneeled to pull him closer, and slipped a hand inside his coat, rubbing her palm against his chest, her other hand pulling his head toward her neck. She felt the warmth of his kiss against her skin, and the firm pull of his hand against the small of her back.

"Shit!" growled Jack as their silhouettes illuminated against the wall of a grocery store. The headlights of two snowmobiles swept across Main Street, bouncing off walls as the machines whined and gathered speed. The drivers gunned their throttles again as they cruised down the next two blocks and eased into the roundabout circling the town center. A jeep came toward them down the other side, its headlights blinding them again before passing them.

"Damn security," spat Jack, shielding his eyes.

"They're just doing their job."

He looked at Nicole, turning up an eyebrow. "No need to be charitable. They could turn the lights down or use the blue filters to dampen the glare. Besides, what do we need cops in this town for? We're hundreds of miles away from any kind of civilization."

Nicole cocked her head in disapproval. "They're not cops. They're security. This place takes a special kind of training. What police academy would be relevant up here? The only law that's relevant is the town's code. You know we need to be careful."

"Yeah, yeah, but so what if someone finds this little bit of hoarfrost."

Nicole looked at Jack, narrowing her eyebrows. "How can you say that, Jack Hackett? You know that would be terrible. This whole village—and your Poppy's livelihood—depends on us keeping this place secret."

"Dad can get a job anywhere. He's a great software engineer."

"Then why does he stay?"

Jack's mood livened up. "Oh, I don't know, maybe 'cause he needed to tutor a child prodigy directly descended from the original Nicholas Klaas?"

"Huh! Or maybe he needed someone to civilize his son."

"Well, judging by last night, I don't think you've been doing a good job of that!"

Even in the evening's darkness, Nicole could see the twinkle in Jack's eye.

Jack sent a cross look at her. "Are you coming over tonight?"

Nicole hesitated.

"Poppy and Ma will be working late," he pressed.

She smiled. "Great! Then I can stay around, and he can teach me more code! Now that I'm going to MIT…." Her own comment took her breath. She said it so naturally, with so much conviction, as if her path had been ordained. "Umm, afterall," she stammered, "I need to learn as much as I can to keep up with all those whiz kids!"

"Ha! Ya think?" Jack grabbed the belt around her waist and pulled her into a narrow alley between two stores. Nicole yelped and then giggled as they disappeared into the shadows.

Later, as they re-emerged onto Main Street, Nicole fidgeted with her pullover sweater buttons after she realized they hadn't lined up correctly. Jack pulled his jacket up to tuck the last tail of his shirt back in his jeans as he fumbled to keep the envelope from falling into the crystalized winter dust. Sheepish eyes darted up and down the street, guilty checks to see who observed their detour.

"At least below the surface of the polar ice cap we don't have blizzards," Nicole said, pulling her windbreaker closer as she snapped two more buttons closed. The chill was creeping back in now that the world wasn't about to end. "We wouldn't last two seconds up there."

Jack squeezed her hand. "Are you coming over tonight?"

Nicole shook her head with a heaviness that seemed to slow her gait. "I've got to talk to Dad. My reckoning is here."

The village seemed to disappear into the background as they walked the next block, neither saying a word and oblivious to passers-by. Nicole felt the warmth of Jack's hand, shifting her fingers to interlace with his, to touch as much of his skin, as she could. Her mind drifted as they meandered past the last of the shops. The drug store seemed empty, holiday card racks revealing gaping expanses between birthdays, condolences, and trite sentimentalities. Jack's birthday sent her into the store last time. She found the perfect card—a banana riding a sleigh down a steep slope with exuberant outstretched stick hands, it's destination three scoops of ice cream at the bottom with whipped cream and a bright red cherry on top that would surely split in two. The words were as stupid as the image: "You split me up! Happy Birthday!" It was corny, but she couldn't stop laughing when she saw it, and she knew Jack would get the joke. He did, of course.

Nicole's mind drifted. Sixth grade. That's when she really got to spend time with him. And Poppy and Ma. And his brother and sister. His mom and dad were dwarfs, like Jack, but he had two sisters that were average sized, like she was. She had never thought that two little people could have average size kids, which seemed odd. Sure her dad was average size and her mom was a dwarf, but it wasn't until she spent time with the Hacketts that she began to think clearly about genetics.

Even now she was perplexed by her inattention to these details as a child. They were so apparent to strangers when she traveled to Florida with her parents. People would stare at them, but she didn't know why. As an only child, she had never noticed the differences in height in their village near the northernmost pole of humanity when they attended games, dinners, or other village events. Those first few times with the Hacketts were the first ones she began to think she was different. But Jack didn't seem to mind. Nor did Dad. Or Mom. Or Jack's parents or sisters.

Nicole's chest seemed to sink as she thought of her mom. Her stays with the Hacketts were brief, at first. Her mom just needed rest, the doctors said. Then, the days-long stays become a week, then two weeks, then by her eighth-grade year, months. But she was falling in love with Jack, so she didn't mind the time away from her parents.

Nicole pulled Jack closer as they walked and let her head fall to rest on the top of his. Two months away from her mom. Now, she wished she could reclaim those days. She remembered the shock of seeing her mother helped off the snowmobile in front of their house, exhausted and weary. This strong, resilient person, was unable to walk up the four short steps to her house without assistance from her dad and an average-sized nurse. The accommodations she had always made for her physical stature were now being adapted to bolster her physical and mental resilience. Nicole had stopped dead in her tracks as she had watched her mother navigate the rise to the porch. Her mom's hug that day, on the porch, would be the strongest she would ever feel or give.

Her throat seemed to seize as she remembered watching her rock become thinner, weaker, and more chiseled with each day. The nurses were attentive and compassionate, steeped in the knowledge of what lay ahead. They tried to explain, in bits and pieces, what they thought a teenager could handle. But she was fourteen. What could she know? And her dad seemed to whither with each pound that her mom lost. Hospice sucked. But the hospice nurses were her mom's guardian angels. They were her dad's archangels. They kept the two of them afloat. Then they were gone. With her mom.

Nicole and Jack slowed to a stop as the sidewalk disappeared into the frost.

******

Jack looked up at Nicole. "Your dad likes me. At least I think he likes me. Do you want me to come in with you?"

"Thank you, Jack, but I think I need to face this myself."

Jack took her hands in his and looked up one more time at Nicole. Her sweet brown eyes stared down at him; her face framed again by new errant wisps of hair poking out from her hat as if to take one last look at a world that would never be the same. "I love you, Nic."

Nicole smiled. "I don't know what I would do without you." She hesitated before turning away. "You know I love you, too, right?"

Jack smiled, lowered his lips to her hands, and lifted his eyes up again. "Of course."

******

Nicole looked at the two-story house, its wrap-around porch sheltered by ornate Victorian eaves that fit the architectural sensibilities of the town, if not the weather. Two small turrets framed the second floor of the house, their sloped cone roofs reaching up just to touch the ice ceiling that protected it from the deadly barren landscape above. Twenty feet below the polar ice cap, the house had little need for shelter or protection from the elements. As long as the hydraulic turbines twenty feet below them kept the ice frozen under their feet, the North Pole was just like any other village cloaked in the darkness of an arctic winter. If the polar winds and ice made it this far down, everyone knew survival was little more than fantasy, much like the myth her father and this town continued to cultivate with art and deliberation. All the North Pole's contingency plans were built on its thirty-six-hour escape window and a collective prayer of faith.

She crossed the street and opened the wrought iron gate hinged to a white picket fence, the same one that opened for her mom nearly four years earlier. The metal seemed to keep the fence intact and complete, giving them, at least symbolically, the privacy of personal celebration, meditation, and... grief.

She could see the warm glow of the first-floor windows, but condensation clouded the view inside. Her father was home. She chuckled to herself. Their engineers could insulate the houses to keep the ice from melting around them, and a village from falling into the Arctic Ocean, but they still hadn't figured out how to keep water from building up on the glass panes of their windows. Well, at least that was one more "normal" feature of living in the village.

Not that it mattered. She knew he would be inside even if she couldn't see him now.

53

Nicole walked up the steps, the bulky envelope, still unopened, tucked under her arm. She pressed her palm against the rectangular pad to the side of the front door. The pad glowed green. Three blue dots appeared, precisely placed to accommodate the particulars of a thumb, middle finger, and pinky finger of an eighteen-year old girl, five foot five inches in height, 130 pounds, with an ancestral Danish physique mixed with a splash of Bohemia, and DNA that included more than a trace of dwarfism. The lights turned from blue to green, and she heard the latch shift. She pressed her hand against the heavy faux wood door, and it opened to let her in.

"Nicole is that you?"

"Duh, I hope so. Otherwise you'd be dead."

She heard the familiar, deep laugh of her father down the hall.

"Well come on back to the kitchen. I'm still making dinner."

Nicole kicked off her boots, snow falling into a grating where it quickly melted and dripped into a drain. She removed her jacket, and lifted it toward a rack, let it rest in mid-air for just a few seconds as she smelled Jack's lingering scent, pulled it against her cheek, and then secured it to an iron hook. She breathed in. She loved the detail of the house. Her mom and dad had custom built it before she was born. The mix of classic Anglo and clean Scandinavian styling kept her senses alive. The art, the drapes, the rugs, the furniture. Mom had made this her home, their home, as her father had built NP Enterprises and her mom had worked freelance with a global marketing firm based in Tallahassee. Nicole was born into this house. It was all she knew. It was as much a part of her as the genes she inherited from her parents.

Nicole looked down at the envelope and started to walk down the hall.

She must have walked this hallway a thousand times over the past three years. Each time she expected to hear her mom's voice. She felt her heart beat a normal meter in her chest at the coat rack. The beat would accelerate into a heavy thump with each step toward the kitchen. She couldn't tame it. Each day, her head told her that her mom was gone. She wouldn't be in the kitchen. She couldn't be in the kitchen. But each foot closer to the kitchen, her mom's sanctuary, seemed to inflame the pressure in her head. A shortness of breath and heaviness in her nose would surface, as if she were emerging from week-long bouts of sobbing. Like after her mother had died and she witnessed the listless life of her father in the months that followed.

After the first year, the doctors resolved that Nicole could no longer be grieving. Her counselors and the psychologist said the road was rough, but she had come out the other side. With time, they said, she would be back to normal. *Normal.* What does that mean when you're an only child? When you lost your rock? When the only more important person in your life than her mom was as shredded inside as you?

Don't worry, the counselors had told her father. She'll be back to normal. Before she went to college, they predicted. Any congestion in the nasal cavities of her head was likely due to allergies, the doctors finally concluded. Allergies. Seriously? Twenty feet below the polar ice cap in a two-square mile ice cave floating on the arctic ocean? What could survive down here that would give her allergies? *Bullshit*, Jack had said.

"Hey, honey, how was school?"

Nicholas Klaas cracked an egg on a cast-iron skillet, letting the yolk and albumen ooze into a sizzling edible potpourri of peppers, new potatoes, onions, and okra.

"Doesn't smell like much," Nicole said.

Her father smirked as he cast a sideways glance to his daughter. He swiped a jar from a shelf nearby. "Behold!" he said triumphantly as green and grey specks scattered across his concoction. "A little oregano. A few crushed Italian herbs. Et voilà!"

She looked at him, amused. "That's French."

Her father twisted his lips and eyebrows, forcing Nichole to smile and shake her head. "Well, what's the Italian?"

"I don't know," Nicole said, shaking her head. "But it looks like you just made something from Latin America and then dressed it up with Italian herbs. Perhaps, *aqui*?"

The older Klaas shook his head in mock disappointment. "Three years of French, four years of Latin."

Her father's beard, speckled with a rich mix of grey and dark browns, had grown out as it usually did this time of the year. His hair was thinning on top, but she looked forward to the ritual shedding of the seasonal beard on January 1st. It marked Ōmisoka, the end of the calendar year, and a personal tribute to the Japanese enthusiasm for gifts, manners, and respect for community. She liked the younger look of the clean-shaven Santa Claus.

Nicole chuckled as she recalled the images of the Jolly Old Santa Claus from myth. She didn't think her father had a fat cell anywhere in his body. Not that he worked out much. He just ate well. Plus, he walked over a mile and half to work and back each day. She thought he and her mother put their house on the edge of town so she would have to work just as much to get anywhere.

No one had yet guessed about his true livelihood when they made their annual sojourns to Florida to establish their residency in the Lower Forty-Eight. He said they had to make their presence official for her to stay enrolled in Florida Virtual School. But she knew he needed the break, like everyone else. Several weeks as a "snowbird," fit in with the bustle of the state's sprawling Gulf Coast. He simply told the other snowbirds that he worked up north and ran a woodworking shop that closed for the winter months. Most simply nodded and went on their way, or created chit chat about how great Florida was and how they could never live up north, or if they did how they were glad they moved south and would never move back. The locals really didn't care, but they were welcoming and embracing regardless of where they said they had come from. After all, who wouldn't love Florida?

Nicole smiled. "All that effort for naught when it counts!"

"Do you want me to add shrimp?"

"Shrimp?"

"Yeah, baby, let's go global! All out! Had the shrimp brought in on a special delivery from Apalachicola just yesterday. Fully stocked at Ed's. Adds a dash of Caribbean. Hmmm. That might mean we add some pork. Or rice. Maybe a bit more pepper...."

Nicole stepped up from behind him and wrapped her arms around his waist. "I think it's going to be fine the way it is."

"Hmm. No shrimp?"

She buried her nose in his back. "No, I think it's perfect."

Nicholas paused as he used a spatula to turn the vegetables. "Okay. We'll sprinkle a little fresh grated Romano cheese over it, and we'll be done!"

A few more minutes, and the two were sitting at their usual kitchen nook. Two plates of food weren't taking long to devour, washed down with crystal-clean filtered water provided courtesy of the Arctic Ocean and the village's state-of-the-art desalination plant.

"You know," Nicole said, "this place is pretty interesting."

"What place?"

"The village. The North Pole. This whole complex."

"Interesting compared to what?"

Nicole shrugged. "The rest of the world, maybe? I think I'm going to miss it."

Her father looked up from his plate. His eyes seemed unfocused, as if remembering a distant memory but unable to give it definition. He turned back to the plate and lifted a fork of vegetables glued together with Romano into his mouth, beginning a slow chew. "So, have you started on your college applications?"

Nicole stabbed a piece of potato with her fork, her plate now a pallet of red peppers, green okra, orange baby carrots, and translucent cooked onions.

"You know, I think you should just get a degree online. I bet Florida State has a great software engineering or computational science program where you could do most of your academic work online. Maybe spend a semester in Tallahassee, but not all your time. That way you could stay here. Work for me. In The Business. I could really use a good, high-level IT person with a knack for management; someone who knows the systems inside and out. Rowdy's a great mentor. I know; Jack has his sights set on Johns Hopkins. At least that's what Rowdy says. But he could use the help. I could use the help. Plus, I would be thrilled to work with you. A father-daughter thing."

Nicole sighed.

"Well," her bearded father nudged. "You've got time. Applications are due March 1st, right?"

"Umm, not quite. Regular admissions apps are due January 1st for MIT and Berkeley, January 6th for Dartmouth. Florida State University has a March 1st deadline, but it's a rolling admission deadline."

Nicholas turned to his daughter, bringing his hand up through his hair. "Oh my God, baby. I am so sorry. I completely missed that. I got so caught up in…. Why didn't you say something? Do I need to call the school to get a college advisor to help you?"

Nicole shook her head. "No need. The school was actually great."

The face behind the beard seemed to freeze. "Was?"

Nicole nodded. She turned around to pull the envelope off the stand. She lifted the package so he could see the logo. "I was accepted."

Nicholas sat still, looking at the package. His shoulders fell, as he sank further into the chair. His fork and knife fell to his plate with a clank against the porcelain. "You haven't opened it."

Nicole diverted her eyes to her own plate of half-eaten food. "I checked online. The size of the envelope just confirms it. Rejections come in a thin letter-size envelope. They only need one sheet to tell you they don't want you." She lifted the envelope and let it drop with a thump on the table top. "If they want you, you've got to fill out a lot more crap."

Nicholas's jaw dropped and his face seemed to slide onto the table top.

Nic jumped up from her chair and wrapped her arms around the neck of the man who had kept her sane her entire life, the other half of the rock that had to become a boulder when her mother passed away in this very house. "I am so sorry, Dad."

Nicholas lifted his fingers to curl around his daughter's hand, closing his eyes as he let his beard rest on her arm. "No need to apologize," he said, his voice quiet and listless. "This is great. MIT's the top engineering school in the world. It's just... it's just... a bit of a shock."

He lifted himself up from the table and grabbed his plate. He looked over at Nicole's plate. "Aren't you going to eat?"

Nichole's eyes blurred with tears. "Dad, I'm not really leaving."

Her father shook his head with a small smile. "Of course you are."

"Not really, I'll be back. This is home."

"Baby, you're leaving. That's just the way it is. I knew the day would come. Your mom and I had so many conversations."

He turned toward the countertop. "Aren't you going to eat?

"I'm not really that hungry."

Nicholas hesitated as he turned toward the sink. "So, I guess you won't be joining me in The Business," he said, facing the wall opposite to Nicole. "I guess you really don't want be in the family business."

"Dad," Nicole said, her voice quivering.

Nicholas dropped the plate on the granite top, a loud crack shooting across the room. He spread both hands on the counter, looking at the wall. "You knew about this before today, didn't you? You've known about this for a while."

Nicole covered an eye with her palm, keeping the tears at bay and breathed in. "I'm sorry, Dad."

Nicholas shook his head.

"I wanted to tell you."

"Then why didn't you?" her father snapped, pivoting to lean against the counter, arms crossed.

Nicole turned her eyes away from his hurt glare. She stammered a few words, but just let her forehead fall to her forearms resting on the table.

"Look," Nicholas said, his voice stern. "I know we prepared you for this. MIT's a great school. The best. I guess... I'm sorry... I'm just not ready to let you go." He threw his hands up in the air. "I mean, what good is all this? What I've built?" He shook his head. "What your mom helped me build?"

Nicole shook her head, tears streaming down her cheeks.

Nicholas shook his head again, diverting his gaze to the stove. "It's okay, Nic. It'll be okay. It's not your problem, Baby. You didn't do anything wrong. In fact, you did everything right." He pulled a kitchen towel from the rack on the stove door, wiped his hands, and started toward the hallway. "I'm sorry, baby." He hesitated, shook his head, and continued toward the door. "I need to go for a walk."

"Dad?"

"Don't worry. I'll be back. I need some fresh air."

Moments later, Nicole heard the door open and then shut with a sharp clack.

Nicole sat at the kitchen table, taking in the empty space, and let go, no longer caring how much she sobbed or if anyone could hear her wails.

******

"I'm so scared," Nicole gasped between tears.

Jack ran his hand over the top of her head, feeling the soft strands of her brown hair as if for the first time as they embraced in the kitchen. "He'll be back. You know he will."

"He's so hurt. You didn't see him. You didn't hear the hurt in his voice. It's like I died and walked out of his life. Just like Mom."

"Well it's not like he can go very far. The entire village is no more than twenty square miles, and the passages to the surface are well guarded. Even Nicholas Klaas can't get out of here without the proper gear and permission from security."

Nicole turned to let her head rest on Jack's shoulder.

"It'll be okay, Nic. He's just going to need time."

Nicole rocked her head forehead on Jack's jacket. "It's too soon, Jack. He can't handle me leaving. It's not fair to him. Maybe I should stay. Tell MIT, 'No.'"

Jack sighed. He pulled back to look at her, cupping Nicole's jaw gently with his hands. "Babe, your dad has been preparing for this for eighteen years. It was the plan. Just like my parents."

"But Mom—" she sniffed.

"Yeah, that sucked. For both of you." Jack's lips opened a toothy smile. "She was great. Remember when she made those chocolate chip cookies in sixth grade? I think it was my first time here."

Nicole giggled. "They were so burned."

"The smoke just hung in the kitchen," Jack laughed.

Nicole lifted her hand to touch Jack's cheek. "And you ate them anyway."

"They were the best chocolate chip cookies I had ever eaten."

Nicole's eyebrows lifted as she grabbed at Jack's ear and tugged it.

"Hey!"

"Don't dis Poppy that way."

Jack nodded as if saying, *You got me there!* "My dad is much better at making cookies, now. Mom depends on them!"

Nicole sighed. "My dad was so hurt. It was like his entire future just disappeared in front of him."

"I guess he's finally confronting the reality, huh."

"Yeah, he's going to be all alone."

"Nic, don't think of it that way." Jack scooted off the chair, letting her hands go, and walked over to the refrigerator. He pulled at a long handle, clearly made to accommodate wide ranges of heights.

"You know," Jack said, pulling a beer from the refrigerator.

"No limes," Nicole called quickly.

Jack looked at her, hesitated. He rolled his eyes, returned the beer bottle, and pulled out a Mountain Dew instead.

"Not much better," she said, smiling.

"Well at least it's legal."

Jack walked back to Nicole and gave her a quick kiss and sat down next to her. "You know, your parents were pretty cool."

"You're not helping," Nicole said.

"Seriously, I don't think I had met a couple that was both average size and dwarf."

Nicole straightened up. "How can that be? Dwarfs are everywhere!" She sat back, remembering her own revelation seeing their stature and Jack's siblings.

"Yeah, but not many in mixed marriages," Jack said. "Of course, they were probably around. I just didn't notice them."

"Well, you couldn't avoid it in this house."

"Nope."

Nicole lifted her hand toward Jack, summoning him to her. She took the bottle out of his hand and placed it on the table. Taking both hands, she pulled him onto her lap so he could straddle her waist and peer directly at her. "I am a lucky girl," she said. She pressed her lips against his and pulled him close as he wrapped his arms around her. "I love you, Jack Hackett."

******

The front door's closing startled Nicole awake. She gasped and started to lift herself before realizing Jack still lay on top of her. "Jack," she hissed. "Dad's home!"

Jack's eyes blinked. "Fuck," he muttered.

Nicole looked into Jack's unfocused eyes as he checked his shirt and pants. "No, we didn't, and we aren't, but I'm not sure you need to be here right now."

"Crap," Jack repeated, shaking his head as if a mat was covering his eyes and his thoughts. He pushed himself up and recognized the living room and couch where they had fallen asleep. "Okay." He rolled off of Nicole, but fell head first onto the floor with a loud thump. "Jesus fucking Christ," he sputtered as he tried to pull his feet out from a blanket that had wrapped around his legs. Nicole smacked his arm. "Sorry, Babe," he said.

"Shhh," Nicole insisted. She put her hands on the top of the couch backing to raise herself, clutching at the wool quilt that had lulled them into a needed slumber. Jack kicked at the cloth sending ripples into the air as one of his knees hit the edge of a coffee table. Jack yelped sending Nicole into a full throttled guffaw. She grabbed at her disheveled shirt and started to grasp at throw pillows. She giggled but couldn't help herself from bursting into another round of laughter.

The light snapped on, revealing Nicholas Klaas towering over the teenagers from the hallway. He crossed his arms, glaring at Jack.

"I'm sorry, Mr. Klaas," Jack said, scampering to his feet, checking his clothes. "Umm, I'm sorry, Mr. Klaas." He looked at Nicole, then back to the most important, most powerful person in the entire village, perhaps the world. "Umm—"

Nicholas remained silent. He looked to Nicole, who was covering her mouth in a miserable attempt to hide her amusement.

"Umm, sorry, Dad."

The elder Klaas didn't smile. "Sorry for what?"

Jack shot a look toward Nicole, whose smile had vanished as she looked at her father.

He stepped toward Nicholas, looking up at him as he approached. "Mr. Klaas…, I am so sorry…. This is all my fault."

Nicholas watched him in silence.

Jack took a deep breath. "Look, when you left—"

Nicholas cocked his head as if challenging Jack to say another word.

"When you left," he continued, "Nic was really upset. She was scared—"

"I invited him over, Dad." Nicole's voice was soft and tender. "I didn't know where you had gone." She sniffed, bringing a finger to her nose, and pulled the quilt closer around her knees and into her lap. She turned her gaze away from her father, the man she cared most deeply about in the whole world. "I didn't know where you went. I was scared. I was upset. So, I called Jack."

"Please, sir, she was really upset. I couldn't leave her alone."

Nicholas lifted his thumb and forefingers to his eyes and began to rub them. He nodded to Jack. "Can you leave me alone with Nicole?"

"Yes, sir," Jack said nodding. He started toward the door but hesitated and turned back toward Nicole. He kissed her on the cheek. "Call me later?" he whispered as she nodded yes.

Jack entered the foyer, put his boots on, and grabbed his jacket from the lower row of the iron hooks above the boot drain. He hesitated, as if preparing to turn back to the living room, but headed out into the night.

******

Nicholas walked into the living room, surveying the carnage of bedraggled quilts and pillows, and a curiously dislodged coffee table. The room was off the hallway, for the most part unused since his wife got sick. He motioned to a top button of Nicole's fleece shirt. Nicole cocked her head, her eyebrows narrowed in confusion. Nicholas tapped a shirt button. Nicole's eyes bulged as she looked down at her blouse and rushed to cover the last of the exposed flesh from her breast. "Dad, we weren't having sex."

Nicholas smirked as he shook his head. "Do you love him?"

"Of course, I love him."

"Then don't pretend you aren't having sex."

65

She looked down at the quilts, lifted her knees, and bunched cloth over and under her thighs. "I just said we weren't having sex when you came in."

Nicholas stepped over to a rocking chair sitting about two feet from the couch. He dropped into the heavily cushioned seat, taking a deep breath. "Your Mom was hot."

Nicole pulled the cloth up to her eyes. "Dad!"

Her father laughed. "Seriously, Nicole, I am glad you have Jack. He's a great kid. You know how I feel about his mom and dad. I've known them both almost my entire life."

She peeked out of the covering. "Thank you."

Nicholas rubbed his hands against his thighs, as if rubbing warmth into them although the temperature inside the house already seemed like it would melt a hole right through the Polar Ice Cap. "Did you know your mom and I wanted more than one child?"

Nicole let the blanket fall from her face, and turned to look at her father. "No. You... she... you didn't tell me."

"Yeah, I wanted five."

Nicole's mouth dropped. "Five?"

Nicholas smiled. "She was definitely not having five! She told me it was easy for me to say, because I wouldn't be home with them. Of course, she worked, too, but we both knew that she would be home with our children. That's just who she was." He moved his hands to the armchair in the rocker and started to tip it back. "But she would have loved three."

"Why didn't you have more? Was I that terrible?"

Nicholas laughed. "No, you were great. In fact, you were sleeping six hours at night by the third month and eight hours by month six."

"Mom didn't get sick until I was ten."

Nicholas nodded. "She had two miscarriages before you were born." He looked directly at Nicole. "You were our miracle baby. The doctors said that now with one baby going to

66

full maturity, Beth was bound to just start churning them out. But she didn't. We tried, but the years just rolled by. Until you were nine years old."

"Nine?"

"That when we first knew something might be wrong. Our hospital up here was good, even back then—lots of talented dwarfs will take a pay cut to work up here—but this is still a small village. We simply don't have a lot of expertise in specialties like oncology. Doc Wright found a mass. He did a biopsy. We decided she needed to go to the Mayo Clinic."

"Is that when I stayed with Mr. and Mrs. Hackett?"

Nicholas nodded.

"I guess I never really knew her when she was well."

"Oh, yes you did." Nicholas nodded as he rocked in the chair. "You knew her when she was well even if you didn't know it. You knew her perhaps at the most important time of your life. At least according to child psychologists and neuroscientists."

Nicole drew in a breath. "I'm afraid I might forget her. I still have the memories of our trips, and our picnics, and working around the table. What if I forget what she looks like?"

The wise father smiled. "Why do you think I keep all these pictures around?"

He looked back to Nicole. "Christmas is when I miss her the most."

Nicole sat up from the couch and walked over to her father, letting herself fall into his lap. She reached around his neck and rested her head on her shoulder. "I love you, Dad. You know that don't you?"

Nicholas kissed the top of her head, and let his arms wrap around his only daughter. "Yes. Just keep telling me, okay?"

Nicole squeezed her arms.

"Nic, I'm glad you have Jack. Not so happy about the profanity, but he's a good guy. And he cares a lot about you. Does he treat you right?"

Nicole nodded. "He's been great. I don't know how I would have gotten through high school without him."

"Baby, I'm sorry I wasn't there for you."

"Dad, it's fine. You had your own shit to go through." She cast a sheepish glance at her father. He either didn't hear the profanity or simply ignored it. "The Hackett's were the best."

"But you needed me."

"We both needed someone. I was angry... at first. I was so scared you would leave me...." She almost said *like Mom* but caught herself. "Your hugs weren't the same. But you were there as much as you could be. I know that. I think it was last year when I realized that your pain... my pain... really was about how much we loved Mom and missed her. And how much we still miss her. I am not sure how long I would have lived my life, how much heartbreak you might have experienced, before I would have realized that. Even though I miss her so much, I am glad I had her for as long as I did."

Nicholas lifted his hand to stroke Nicole's hair. "I guess we all need to grow up."

"Are we growing up, or moving on?"

Nicholas nodded, and smiled. "Both."

They sat for several minutes, taking in the air, the images, the decor of the house Mrs. Klaas built. "I guess it's time to update the house a bit."

Nicole's head nodded as she reached over to clutch his shirt.

Nicholas stroked his daughter's hair. "I'll get an interior designer to take a look."

"Will you remake the house?"

Nicholas sighed. "Nope. We need to rebuild our house, but not tear down our memories." He waited several moments, as if gathering the courage to ask the next question. "When did you find out about MIT?"

"Six twenty-eight pm, December 15th."

"Six twenty-eight pm?"

"Double the value of Pi, the ratio of the diameter of a circle to its circumference."

Nicholas's laugh was so big, so consuming, Nicole couldn't resist joining him as they embraced.

"Perfect," he said, beaming at his daughter.

If you would like to find out what happens at the North Pole after Nicole graduates read:

St. Nic Inc

Available in paperback and eBook form.

Follow Sam at:
(www.srstaley.com)
blog (http://blog.srstaley.com)
Facebook (https://www.facebook.com/srstaleyfiction)
Twitter (@SamRStaley)
Instagram (samuelrstaley)

Neon Holiday

Saundra G. Kelley

Happy Holidays! Merry Christmas! Happy Hanukah! Felice Novidad. As the old song goes, "It's the hap-happiest time of the year..." but not necessarily for me.

Please don't get me wrong, I love shopping, gift-giving, singing carols, and being with family as much as anyone, but I can't get into the holidays when I'm supposed to. The reason might be the nature of my work: I'm a contract window and vignette designer for some of the better stores in Atlanta. Planning for those visual stories begins in July, with the finished sets revealed the week prior to Thanksgiving. The Monday immediately after, I switch gears, moving to decorating historic homes for Christmas. Then I go into hiatus until the middle of January when things ramp up for Valentine's Day.

My carriage house apartment, well within walking distance of the downtown shopping district, sits atop the four-car garage of a restored Victorian mansion. My studio window has a perfect view of the tree-lined avenue below. I'd call it idyllic if it weren't so damned quiet—sort of like a cemetery for the not-quite-dead.

After the holiday decorations were up, my life was again my own. I could go shopping, splurge on good food, popcorn, and old movies—whatever I wanted. *Sabrina*, starring Audrey Hepburn was the hands-down favorite. After all, I, too, lived in a carriage house and dreamed of finding love. Regrettably, there were no handsome brothers to flirt with at the big house, only a wealthy widow.

Those old movies provided inspiration for some of my window designs. Few things inspire me more than snuggling down on the window seat with my favorite pen and a pad of good paper after watching a classic film. By the time February rolls around, the walls of my studio are plastered with designs.

I was watching *Casablanca* one evening when a sharp knock on the door brought me up with a start. It was my charming landlady.

"Suzanne, (pronounced with three syllables) I hate to interrupt you, but my nephew, Daniel Hickcok, is coming to stay with me for the holidays. I will introduce you properly but in case I'm not here when he arrives, I want you to know there'll be a new vehicle in the garage. I hope his comings and goings don't disturb you."

It was a surprise—she seldom had guests, so I was glad she told me. Up till then, only her lavender Cadillac and my restored '47 Ford pickup occupied the garage, not including her grandfather's old buggy. "Thanks for letting me know, Mrs. Bostick," I answered with a smile. "I'll watch out for him."

"I appreciate it, dear," she said, looking at me over the rims of her purple-rimmed glasses. "I expect the two of you will get along simply fine. I must go now. The Daffodils, my garden circle, are meeting in my parlor in an hour."

Before she left, Mrs. Bostick turned back to look at the walls still covered with this years' holiday designs. "My dear, those are your best yet. I cannot wait to go downtown to see them in person. Perhaps Daniel will go with me."

She caught me off-guard. "Daniel? Oh, you mean your nephew, don't you?" But the lady was already at the foot of the stairs, rushing to her meeting.

Later in the day, when the traffic died down, I went to my storage unit to check on the inventory and then to Macy's to measure the window dimensions again. Everything I needed for the sets had to be in place before anything went up. Entering the empty set with the lights dimmed, I began taping kraft paper to the windows. Without it, I'd never get anything done for curious watchers. Discovering I needed an antique halter for the life-sized horse and the right trunk for the carriage, I planned a trip to the antiques district the next day.

Though I was accustomed to being stared at while I did this, I became acutely aware of someone watching me. Turning, I saw a low-slung motorcycle stopped in traffic parallel to the display window. The rider, who casually leaned against the seat, was looking straight at me. Long and lean like his bike, wearing a black leather jacket with his cap turned backward, he could have been one of thousands of bikers in Atlanta, but there was something about him that struck me. When the light changed, he moved with the traffic, but not before tipping his cap in my direction. Purple neon lights flickered in his wake.

Finishing up and more than a little distracted, I drove over to the Peachtree Center to do some last-minute shopping on the Temporaries floor. I got what I needed, then pulling out of the underground parking garage I saw lavender lights in the distance. Distracted, I turned the wrong way.

Realizing the mistake almost immediately did me no good; it was a one-way street! Before I knew it, I was in the twilight zone and completely disoriented. I recognized nothing. Roiling fog rose in the darkness from uneven cobble stones. Strange heads wearing Edwardian hats popped up from the drains under the manhole covers. Odd children dressed from another era wondered around untended and there were horse-driven carriages rolling along under gaslights.

Where the heck was I? In one of my set designs?

Slowing down to a crawl for fear of running the children over or squishing a popping head, I was searching for a place to turn around when a man ran in front of the car with his arms out.

"Cut! Cut! How in the hell did *you* get in here?"

Was he cursing at me?

"This is a movie set," he yelled. "I'm losing money by the second. Somebody, get this dammed woman and her car off my set."

Forgetting my confusion, my temper lit like fresh kindling. I came to a full stop and stepped out of the car to confront the man.

"The last time I checked, this was a public street. A KEEP OUT sign and a barrier would have helped," I yelled back. "If somebody will show me the way out, I'll be more than happy to oblige."

My response seemed to cool him down until he realized his cast and crew were laughing at his expense. Angry again, he stomped away leaving me an opportunity to study the situation. The cast members were dressed in outlandish holiday costumes with bizarre face paint beginning to melt in the heavy fog. Set against downtown's Christmas decorations and holiday music, they presented a dystopian universe I rather liked, especially when I noticed one of my store windows nearby.

One of the crew members showed me the way out. No longer angry, I was elated—my work might serve as a backdrop in a movie! *How cool was that!* I drove away in my little red truck singing "White Christmas" at the top of my lungs.

The night, however, was not finished with me. Just ahead in the left-turn lane, a low-slung bike with the purring engine of a retrofitted Harley-Davison slipped in front of me like greased lightning. It was the bike with the purple neon undercarriage I'd seen earlier...

When I pulled up behind him, he turned back to grin at me and sped ahead. Something about him put me in mind of a wolf, but it wasn't frightening. Instead, it was alluring.

Without thinking, I grinned in recognition then wondered at the wisdom. Surely seeing him several times in one night was a coincidence. I would never see him again.

Feeling in the holiday spirit, I was singing with the radio when I pulled my old truck into the garage. By long habit, I prepared to turn into my parking space only to discover it occupied by a familiar motorcycle. It was the Harley that I'd seen several times that day with a black leather cap positioned on the seat.

Exhausted, I climbed the stairs, took a bath, and crawled into bed. When sleep finally came, lavender lights and dancing manhole covers haunted my dreams.

******

The next morning was installation day so there was no time to waste on the alien presence below. Was my downtown Harley rider the nephew she told me about?

From the top of the stairs I saw the imposing presence was still tucked into my space, black cap and all. Curious, I touched the soft leather bringing it to my face to inhale his scent before returning it to the seat.

Bemused, I picked up the trunk and bridal at Anderson's antiques and went to work. With one more window to finish, my day was fully booked. When I finally yanked the brown paper away from the windows at sundown, stepped away and turned the set lights on, an audience was waiting with applause at the ready. It was always like that, and the best Christmas gift I could ask for.

When I got home, the bike was in the garage, but it had moved to a different spot. A note on the door from Mrs. Bostick asked me to come over as soon as possible.

Wondering what was up, I showered quickly and dried my dark hair. Letting it hang full and loose, I dressed in a black turtleneck and jeans. The back light was on at the house, so after knocking, I entered through the mud room. Mrs. Bostick was in the dining room having coffee with someone. At my entrance, she rose as did the tall man seated to her right.

"Oh, my dear, you've come! Suzanne Woods, let me introduce you to my nephew, Daniel Hickock."

It *was* him—the man on the Harley. My heart stopped beating when he moved toward me with his hand out. Since I was apparently unable to extend it, he took my hand in his saying, "We've already met, haven't we? Would you care to have breakfast at Savannah's Place in the morning? We need to talk."

With his aunt eagerly watching the dance play out between us, I said yes.

Follow Saundra Kelley

https://saundrakelley.com/

https://www.facebook.com/AppalachianStorytellers

Other books by Saundra G Kelley

The Day the Mirror Cried
Danger in Blackwater Swamp
Danger on Roan Mountain

Moving On: A Christmas Story

Diane Sawyer

I know that I need to make changes in my life. Christmas is only a few weeks away so it's too soon to make New Year's Resolutions. I don't need to change anything about my career. That's the highlight of my life. I am a translator working with communications in French, Spanish, and Italian for a large international business. Their American office is located in downtown St. Petersburg, Florida. This is the city where I have lived most of my adult life and the city I love. Maybe *dream job* is a better description of my work. Besides the usual translations and correspondence, I have the opportunity to attend conferences in person and online where I meet interesting people. My supervisors are very generous. However, the rest of my life is not as satisfying as my career. I haven't had a date in more than two years. There are some very nice men at the office, but I was always rushing in and out to keep up with my responsibilities as a homeowner. I am sure I gave the impression that I wasn't interested in a social life. Yet nothing could be further from the truth.

The three-bedroom fixer-upper home with a large yard that I bought ten years ago took up every free moment of my time; trim the hedges, clean out the garage, rake the leaves, sweep the driveway, mow the lawn, get rid of the weeds, clean the gutters, and wash the windows. Maintaining the house and yard took 100% of my *free* time. That left me no time to socialize and perhaps date. Lack of dating a nice guy has really begun to bother me. I can't deny what I know for sure; I'm missing a huge part of life that my friends and colleagues enjoy. I have no time to meet people, get together with friends, and in general, enjoy life.

When I finally made up my mind to sell the house, I met with a real estate agent. He made suggestions, like decorate the windows and yard and make necessary improvements, such as painting, repairing the driveway, and replacing the garage door. I admitted I didn't have time for all that, but I would do what I could. He shook his head and said with a frown, "Let's see what happens, but don't expect a miracle. That only happens in movies and books, not real life."

After looking for a more care-free home, I chose a one-bedroom apartment with a "bonus room" that would be perfect as an office or library, and also a place to exercise when it was raining or too hot to go outdoors. The apartment was on the top floor of a five-story building with a beautiful view. It was situated across from a park with walking trails and tennis courts, plus a white sandy beach and palm trees. Too good to be true. Since it was a rental apartment, I would not have the responsibilities that went with owning a home. Like my current home, it was only a twenty-five-minute commute to work. I signed the lease, stared at my name, Donna Jackson—same name, but possibly a new lifestyle would be coming soon. I told myself not to give in to indecision. I wanted to move. I would soon have a better life. It was up to me to meet people and pursue a social life.

Reality set in as I hired a mover to transport my belongings and the tagged pieces of furniture and boxes to the apartment. He commented, "Moving all this so close to Christmas?" What was I thinking? Sell a home with Christmas only two weeks away. No one was going to buy a home with the holiday so near. Everyone would be planning to decorate their home and yard, shop for gifts, write Christmas cards, plan menus, and possibly entertain out-of-town visitors.

With help from my friends, I moved in that weekend. Before the day was over, I had met many neighbors and accepted invitations to two parties. I was happy with the way things were going.

Two days later, the realtor called to say that a couple with three children had made an acceptable offer on my house. Not great, but acceptable. I liked that word. I accepted the acceptable offer and was certain that my life had just taken a turn for the better. I decided to celebrate by buying outdoor furniture for the balcony of my apartment and splurging on two dozen potted plants to make the balcony inviting, a place to rest and relax, enjoy crossword puzzles, and read. I was shedding the old world of rush-rush-rush and work-work-work and beginning my new life with more options such as enjoying, relaxing, and spending leisure time with my friends. Leisure was a word I rarely had occasion to use.

The next day at the office, I sat down at my desk and organized my day. I found myself smiling, knowing that I was free from all the chores that my home had required. I even began to sing softly to myself. "Jingle Bells" was the tune that escaped from my lips. Suddenly, I felt the presence of someone standing in front of my desk.

"Hello," the man said. "I was hoping to find you here, not at a meeting."

"Can I help you? Did you have a question about your report that I translated?" I asked. I couldn't imagine why else he would be at my desk. He had never spoken to me before now.

"No. It's more personal than that. I know your name is Donna Jackson. I'd like to get to know you better and know more about you," he said.

He moved closer to my desk. "My name is Tim Cassidy." He shook hands with me. "One good thing about Christmas," he said. "It brings people together. I'm having a party on Christmas Eve at my house. Friends and colleagues and neighbors will be there. Can I count on your coming to the party?" He handed me an invitation.

I hesitated, then took the invitation and put it in my purse. "Yes. I'll be there," I said. Wow. My life was definitely changing or maybe I was changing. I couldn't wait to step into the new life and the new me.

"Good. Seven o'clock," he replied and flashed a winning smile.

Who could say *no* to a smile like that and such a nice invitation? He was one of the lawyers who made sure that none of the contracts contained loopholes and that everything in a foreign language had been translated into English. Those contracts were eventually sent to me to make sure the language was translated correctly. But this was the first time Tim Cassidy and I had ever spoken, and it wasn't about work. And he initiated the conversation. Yes, my life was absolutely changing. I took a few minutes going through my desk drawer to find a list of employees and pertinent information. According to the file, Tim Cassidy had two teen-age daughters in college. The family home was in St. Petersburg. No other pertinent information was included. There was no mention of a wife.

******

Three days later when I came home from work, I heard my landline phone ringing.

"Hello," I said.

"Hello, Miss Jackson," a young woman's voice said. "I am Tim Cassidy's daughter, Annie. My sister Beth is here with me. Could we come over and speak to you for ten minutes or so?

Our father doesn't know we are doing this, so we hope you can keep a secret."

"Yes, please come right over," I said, wondering what this was all about and why it was a secret.

"We will be there in a few minutes. We parked nearby. Thank you."

The doorbell rang and I hurried to open the door, wondering what this could be all about. I love mysteries, the ones in novels, but this was real life, and I didn't have a clue about what to expect. After quick introductions, we sat down in the living room.

"Please tell me what's on your mind," I said. Even if Annie hadn't told me that she and Beth were Tim Cassidy's daughters, I would have figured it out. Both girls had his good looks, mesmerizing eyes, and fabulous smile.

Annie inched forward on the couch. "Beth and I have something to tell you. Let me begin by letting you know that our mother passed away three years ago..."

"I am so sorry," I said and wondered where this conversation was going.

Annie continued, "Our father hasn't been on a date since then. He thinks it will be disloyal if he is spending time with another woman. Yes, he is hooked on that word-choice, "another woman." Beth and I want him to be happy.... We want him to have a social life. Right now, it's all work, work, work. Beth and I are in college. He's all alone. And when we are home, we don't really require much care, so he isn't tied down by us. He could have a social life if he wanted to and if he took the initiative."

Beth said, "We asked him, 'Who is the most interesting person at work? Is there someone he might like to share an evening with? Your name came up. No other name was mentioned. Dad admitted he had never had a conversation with you but everyone said complimentary things about you. They had even suggested that he should invite you to the Christmas party at our home. He admitted to us that he was unsure of your response. He was so nervous that we thought he would back off and let the opportunity pass him by."

I knew that syndrome all too well. I thought the sisters were giving him good advice, but if he is keeping himself so busy that he doesn't have time for a social life, he will always be too busy. I had to admit to myself that I was describing myself as well as him. Could be that the girls didn't judge their father fairly. I didn't know the girls of the father enough to make any judgement.

Annie chimed in. "I suggested that Dad have a date for dinner with you some evening before the party so that you could get to know each other better. He said that was too short notice. I said, 'Ask her and see what she says.' He gave us a few arguments, but he admitted that he would like a better social life. I didn't tell him the undeniable truth; his social life was zero, zilch, absolutely non-existent. Deep down, he knew that. His friends were telling him that too."

******

Several days later, I was home from work, reading the mail and figuring out what to have for dinner when my home phone rang.

I picked up and said, "Hello."

"Hello, Donna. This is Tim Cassidy. Is this a good time for you to talk?"

"Yes, this is a very good time for me," I said, hoping I sounded eager, not desperate.

He said, "I know this is short notice, but I was hoping you would agree to have dinner with me tomorrow night at a nice quiet restaurant."

I liked what I was hearing even though I was quite sure his daughters had probably talked him into calling me.

"Yes," I said. "I am free tomorrow night and I would like to have dinner with you."

"Good. I'll pick you up at 7:45."

"My address is—"

"I know where you live. I found your new address in a personnel file."

"Good," was the only response I could come up with.

"See you tomorrow night," he said.

For all the times I had imagined what it would be like to have a man interested in me, I was groping for the right words to say.

"Looking forward to seeing you," was the best I could come up with.

"Good," he said, obviously as stumped as I was for a good response and the phone clicked off.

I sat there wondering if I had imagined all of this, or was I actually going on a date with Tim Cassidy tomorrow night. I got up, went to my closet, and looked through my dresses to find just the right one. I had a pretty red dress that was quite flattering. Should I save that one for the party or wear it for our dinner date? This was an unfamiliar dilemma to me. Wear the red dress to dinner I finally decided. If we don't have a nice time, I could skip the party. Just in case, I found a second choice, a dark green clingy dress that was flattering. I had never worn it because it was too dressy for any place I went. Okay. The green dress for the party, the red dress for dinner.

I went to bed and dreamed sweet dreams.

Early the next morning, I got out of bed and immediately wondered if that telephone conversation was real or if I had dreamed all of that? No. It was definitely real. The red dress and the green dress were resting on a chair, ready to go on a date with Tim Cassidy, on separate evenings of course. "Hooray!

Merry Christmas," the red dress and green dress practically shouted at me. Actually, it was me calling out to the dresses.

I kept myself busy all day at work. Was the clock on the wall always this slow? Was my watch slow too? Finally, the workday ended and I drove home. The moment I entered my apartment the phone rang. I thought Tim had changed his mind. I expected him to say, "We're not going to dinner. I have to cancel all my plans. I am truly sorry. I was looking forward to dinner with you." But it wasn't Tim.

"Hey, Donna," a woman said. "We haven't met yet. I'm your neighbor, Annie, my apartment is three doors away from your door. I'm on the social committee. Since you are new, you probably didn't receive the notice about the Christmas party in the Community Room of our apartment building. It will be held the day after Christmas because many people had plans for Christmas day. We've been doing this for years and it's very popular." She added, "Everyone is asked to bring snacks or treats. There will be entertainment too. Extra copies of the notice are on the table in the community room."

"Thank you," I said. I'll see you there." As a last-minute thought, I asked, "May I bring a guest?"

She said, "Yes."

I breathed a sigh of gratefulness that Tim hadn't canceled the plans for dinner. I had better find out everything that goes on at the community-room party so that I can tell Tim all about it and invite him. Or maybe I needed to slow down. I could scare him off with three dates in such a short time.

The next evening at 7:45 there was a knock at the door. I glanced in the mirror and decided my red dress really looked good. I would even go so far as to say that it made me look good. Tim had never seen me all dressed up, hair perfectly coiffed, pretty jewelry, three-inch heels. He was about six feet tall, and these three inches gave me a good height in case we danced. I really hoped we would dance. I don't remember the last time I danced, but I remember how much I loved dancing.

I opened the door. "Hi Tim," I said.

"Hi Donna." He stepped inside and held out a box of candies. "Sweets for the sweet new person in my life," he said and handed me the candies.

"Thank you," I said, surprised at his calling me 'the sweet new person in his life'. He was no longer as shy as when he spoke to me last. "You are so thoughtful. How did you know I liked chocolate?"

"Lucky guess," he said. "And guess what? I now know we have something in common. We both like chocolate." He checked his watch. "Shall we go?"

"Sure," I said and grabbed my purse. We walked into the beautiful balmy evening. He opened the car door for me. Soon we were on our way to Chez Paris, one of the finest restaurants in town. Many pronounced it Chez Paree, giving it a bit of authenticity and sophistication.

After we were seated and Tim ordered champagne for two, he turned to me and said, "Does the name of this restaurant mean anything special to you?"

"Hmmmm. Chez Paris," I said, pointing at the name on the menu. "Nothing special that I can think of."

He smiled and said, "It makes me think of that famous line in the movie *Casablanca* with Humphrey Bogart and Ingrid Bergman."

"I never saw the movie, but I've heard a lot about it. What line are you thinking of?" I asked, hoping he would talk more now than he did at work.

"I'll fill in some of the story so I can work up to the great line. Here goes. They were in Paris and very much in love. They were sad that they were going to be apart because of the war and facing the awful truth that this might be the last time they would be together. Bogart, hoping to cheer up Bergman about the wonderful time they had enjoyed in Paris, came out with the classic unforgettable line, "We'll always have Paris." And many women in the theater burst out crying because the scene was so heartbreaking. It implied that this was the last time the characters played by Bogart and Bergman would ever see each other again."

"I'm going to rent that movie," I said. "I've heard so much about it."

The waiter poured the champagne. Tim raised his glass and clinked it against mine and said, "You always see this in movies: clinking champagne glasses and the star of the movie saying something romantic. So here goes." He clinked his glass against mine again and said, "Maybe Bogart and Bergman would always have Paris, but you and I will always have this restaurant, Chez Paris."

Before I knew it, I was smiling and enjoying myself and I could see the same was true for Tim. And that funny line of his, "We will always have Chez Paris" really impressed me. Clever and cute... just like Tim himself.

"How about a dance? The band sounds very good," he said.

"Sure. I love to dance," I said.

We walked hand in hand onto the dance floor. We danced two dances.

"That was so nice," I said.

"There's a reason it was nice," he said as we headed back to our table. "I haven't danced in years, but my daughters said I just needed practice. They moved the living room furniture out of the way and took turns dancing with me. They said I was good enough to ask my date to dance. Naturally, that date would be you. So here we are dancing and guess what? My daughters were right. Practice is what I needed. I enjoyed our dancing. You and me, not my daughters and me."

"I enjoyed it too," I said.

"Good," he said. "This is my first date in years and I wanted it to be perfect."

"And?"

"And it's perfect for me. How about for you?"

"It's perfect for me too," I said and smiled.

The evening seemed to fly by. I was so glad I had agreed to go out with him. "This is great," I said. "A nice quiet break before the hectic Christmas activities."

I couldn't hold back. I blurted out, "Would you like to go with me to a Christmas party the day after Christmas? It's in the community room at the apartment building where I live. It won't be fancy like this, but I think it could be fun. I hear that they sing Christmas carols, and they have entertainment and food."

"Sure, I'd like to go," he said.

"Good. I'll get the details to you as soon as I can."

"Okay," he said. "Just you and me or would you like my two daughters to come too? They admitted that they were setting me up with you. Here's the funny part. I was glad to go along with their plans. I just didn't have the nerve to ask you."

I was stunned. "Why?" I asked.

"It was awkward. I thought you might be seeing someone."

I wrinkled my brow. "What would make you think that?"

"Look in the mirror," he said. "You're pretty. Look at the work you turn out for the firm. You're intelligent. If I'm not mistaken, they call that 'beauty and brains.' That definition fits you perfectly. And then let's not forget there is your pretty smile. That's what really won me over."

I couldn't believe what I was hearing. "Oh," was all I could think of to say. Then I came to my senses. "Since I can't guarantee what the party at my apartment house will be like because this will be my first time. Let's just the two of us go. Are you okay with that?"

"Sure. By the way, there's one more thing I can share with you. It's about you."

"Go ahead. I'm listening."

"The guys at work have fantasies about you."

I laughed. "You're making that up."

"No. I imagine many guys at work and elsewhere have asked you for a date."

"You have a good imagination," I said.

Finally, Tim said, "We'd better leave. They are going to turn off the lights and lock the doors."

"Okay," I said.

He drove me home and walked me to the door. We held hands and walked very slowly. I imagined that he didn't want the evening to end any more than I did. Following up on that, I said, "Would you like to come in for a nightcap?" That was a line I had heard spoken in many romantic movies. It went well with the dialog we'd been having throughout the evening.

Tim checked his watch and said, "I wish I could come in, but tomorrow morning I will be meeting very early with a bike group. We ride for two hours, but because of the heat we start at six o'clock, like A.M. Maybe another time."

"That would be very nice," I said. I wanted to add, "I have a bicycle," but I didn't want to push him into something more than he might have wanted.

He put his arms around me and drew me close. We kissed. It was a lovely kiss, a perfect ending to a perfect evening. He murmured in my ear, "I'm glad you said, 'yes,' when I asked you out."

"What choice did I have?" I asked. "It's all part of the Christmas spirit to be nice and understanding to someone, especially on the first date."

"Well then, have a very Merry Christmas," he said. "And may the spirit of Christmas embrace you whenever we are together."

"See you soon," I said. "At work, at parties, on the dancefloor, and other places we haven't yet explored."

"I am looking forward to it all," he said. "Don't forget the party at my house is coming up soon."

"I didn't forget. I'll be there," I said and started to go inside.

"Wait a minute," he called out and I turned around and came back.

"There's one more opportunity for us to spend some time together," he said.

"What did you have in mind?" I asked.

"Bowling. I'm in a bowling group."

"I don't know what I was expecting, but it wasn't bowling. I like to bowl, but I'm not very good at it," I said.

"You should come and join us and enjoy the camaraderie. It's a bunch of guys and gals. None of us are very good so you'll fit right in."

"I'm not sure if I've been complimented or insulted, but yes, I'll go bowling with you. Give me the details, the time and place."

"It's the Sunshine Bowling Alley. Tuesday mornings is when we usually meet next, but we are taking off until after Christmas. The bowling alley isn't far from here. You should know we meet very early—at 6:30 in the morning. Coffee and donuts and lots of laughs." He flashed that winning smile. "I'll get you a team shirt so you will feel like one of the group. The logo on the shirt is 'We love bowling.' Not very original. And each shirt has the person's name. Can you see it now? D-O-N-N-A."

"Perfect," I said.

I went back inside, closed the door behind me, and collapsed on the couch. Bowling! That was an experience I hadn't counted on. I still couldn't believe how wonderful the evening was, how wonderful Tim was. The Christmas spirit had lulled us both into a perfect evening!

Several days passed and I put on the green dress and called Uber to drive me to the Christmas party at Tim's house. From outside it sounded like the house was full of people. Tim welcomed me at the door. I met too many people to remember the names. Everyone was having fun. Most were neighbors. Some were friends from a neighborhood where Tim and his wife used to live. Others were members of clubs. Tim's work friends were there and his bike friends and bowling friends too. Tim's daughters, Beth and Annie, came over to welcome me, and I was glad to see them. Beth whispered to me, "You and Dad are perfect together."

Annie added, "Thank you for making Dad so happy." Next, she said, "When Dad is happy, we are happy."

Beth jumped back into the conversation and said to me. "Thank you for rescuing our dad from a life of loneliness and regret. As you can see from all the people here that Dad has friends. But until now he didn't have a special person, someone to date."

Annie said, "We like talking to Dad again now that he's got some really fun things to tell us. He's been walking around in a daze for three years. Now he's coming back to us thanks to you."

Tim circulated among the crowd and spent time with me too. "I'll be back in a minute," he said to me. "I need to attend to some host duties. I'll have the bartenders bring out more ice."

He was only gone for a minute when a woman came up to me and said, "I'm curious. How do you know Tim?"

"We work at the same company," I said.

"Really," she commented with a sarcastic tone. "It looked like something else was going on. It looked like you were paying attention to him as if he were the only man in the room. And of course, he seemed to return the favor, and he paid a lot of attention to you. What choice did he have? He's a perfect gentleman. Apparently, you thought he was truly interested. Well, think again."

"What's this all about?" I asked her.

"I'm interested in Tim. I've known him for quite a while, and I'm hoping that the interest is mutual. He's a really good catch." She added, "I'm going to leave you now after I say goodnight to him. Think about what I've told you. Consider him taken, as in T-A-K-E-N." After spelling out the word, she turned and left before I could say anything, although I didn't have a clue what I could possibly say to her.

A sing-along of Christmas carols began and then the daughters' friends from a choral society performed for the guests. It was lovely, a classic celebration.

As time passed, people began to leave.

Tim left to say thanks to the people who were leaving. The team members that shared an office with Tim stopped to say hi to me. One of them, whose nametag said SAM, stepped away from the group. "You don't know us," he said, "but we are on Tim's team at work. He's a great guy and from what he says, you are a very special person." This is a wonderful season filled with happiness and good cheer so I guess it's true that timing is everything. "Merry Christmas... and make the most of it," he said and left.

Many were leaving. I said to Tim, "Thank you for inviting me to the party. You have two nice daughters and you have many good friends. I'm going to leave but I wanted to say Thank you for the wonderful evening. It was a great party. I called Uber and a car is on the way." He walked me to the door. I said, "Goodnight," to the daughters.

Tim said, "Goodnight, Donna. I'm looking forward to seeing you soon."

I got into the Uber car and had several minutes to think.

I started my new life only a short time ago, but it was the best decision I had ever made. I had wanted a more social and more relaxing and more fun way of living, but I never realized I was looking for love, that love was missing from my life. The way I had lived I was always busy with a house and yard. I made time for a career that I enjoyed but I had no time to pursue love. Children know that they should tell their parents and write notes to Santa naming what they want for Christmas, but adults, at least me, don't state what they want. In my case I didn't even admit to myself that I was looking for love. Apparently, some children, like Tim's daughters, know how to make someone's dreams come true, and that's a wonderful trait, especially when that someone is me.

About the Author

Diane Sawyer grew up in Greenport, Long Island. She graduated from SUNY at Albany, Seton Hall University, and Fordham University, where she received a Ph.D. She now resides in St. Petersburg, Florida. Her short stories have won awards. Her novels have been published internationally. She is a frequent guest speaker at writing groups and workshops.

Previous works at SYP Publishing - Mystery

The Tell-Tale Treasure

Trouble in Tikal

When not writing, Diane volunteers as a docent at the Dalí Museum. She also serves as Secretary of the Friends of the South Community Library in St. Petersburg. Diane loves fitness, adventure traveling, meeting people, and spending time with her family.

CPSIA information can be obtained
at www.ICGtesting.com
Printed in the USA
LVHW011305191220
674520LV00005B/790

9 781596 161160